Running from the Prince

JULIA KEANINI

PICKLED PLUM PUBLISHING

Pickled Plum Publishing

Cover Design by Melody Jeffries Design

For my sweet Mika.

<h1 style="text-align:center">One</h1>

"You've got to be kidding me," Alex said amid the sighs, gasps, and even an outright scream of one of her colleagues.

"Even *I* didn't see that one coming," Jane, Alex's friend/bodyguard, said with wide eyes.

Alex slid down in her auditorium seat as the man she'd refused to marry took the last seat on the platform of judges who would determine her future. Okay, maybe marry was a bit strong, but he'd asked to court her, and in their world that came right before marriage and was nearly as bad of a refusal. She could practically hear fate laughing at her.

"He's the brooding, hot one, right?" Nadine, a girl sitting in the row in front of Alex, asked Lori, who was sitting beside her.

"Aren't they all?" Lori said as she and Nadine began to giggle.

The Valdorian Princes. There wasn't a woman between the ages of five and ninety-five who hadn't swooned over at least one of them. Except for maybe Alex. No, she was giving herself a bit too much credit. She'd definitely swooned over all of them, but marrying the eldest? That was a whole different story. If anyone knew the kind of life a queen led, it was Princess Alexandra

Torre. And that was part of the reason why she was now sitting in an overcooled auditorium with a group of one hundred twenty-somethings vying for ten coveted spots as interns for world-renowned photographer, Jacques Ledoux.

"It's Prince Theo," Emmalee, the third member of the giggling trio, said as she sat up a bit straighter. Maybe she was belatedly remembering the fact that she was not a teenaged groupie at her first boy band concert. Emmalee, Alex's biggest competition in the intensive, one-year photography course she'd fought tooth and nail to be a part of, wasn't the type to lose her head or her drive.

But a quick glance around the room told Alex Emmalee wasn't alone. Every woman in the room had been reduced to teenaged groupie status. Alex fought the urge to roll her eyes.

What was he doing here?

Alex knew *she* couldn't be the reason. One, she was sure he wasn't too broken up that she'd refused to court him. The whole thing had been arranged by their parents after all. And two, he couldn't know that she'd be here. She had worked for almost six full months to come up with the alternate persona that she'd become during Jacques Ledoux's photography course. Thanks to help from her eldest brother, Mando, she hadn't only changed her name to Alex Turner, she had a brand-new passport, identity, and had even become a graduate of Wilson High School in Alabama. But she'd drawn the line when Mando offered to fake her a degree from a university. She hadn't earned a degree, neither as Alexandra Torre nor as Alex Turner, and she wouldn't allow her connections to give her that advantage, although every other participant in her program had a college degree of some sort. She wanted to get into Jacques's program on her merit alone. And she had.

Alex saw Theo glance around the room, bringing her attention back to the man and her question. She turned her head to Jane even though she knew Theo wouldn't be able to recognize her with her dyed blond hair, nothing like the mane of dark hair she used to sport. On top of that, her pale complexion was far from her normally tanned skin, thanks to the fact that she'd kept out of the sun for the last year and a half. Also, her face was free of any kind of makeup, and she wore a pair of wide rimmed glasses that were not a necessity considering Alex's twenty/twenty vision. With her long hair pulled back into a simple braid, Alex Turner was the antithesis of everything Alexandra Torre had been. Alex wore Converse and graphic T's, leaving all of her fancy dresses, starched blazers, and pencil skirts back in the castle that had been her home.

"He's staring at you," Jane muttered, and Alex felt her heart speed up. Could he see past her disguise?

"He's definitely eyeing you," Lori said to Emmalee, and Alex didn't have to look at the woman to know the self-satisfied look that must be covering her face. Alex had seen that smile enough times when Jacques had dished out praise to Alex's gorgeous nemesis. Emmalee wasn't alone in the praise she received, but to hear her talk about it, no one else in the program was nearly as beloved by Jacques as she was.

Alex glared at Jane. She'd gotten Alex's hopes up, no not her hopes, she didn't want to attract Theo's notice, but her heart had been racing nonetheless. It was racing because she didn't want to be found out, not by the fact that the gorgeous prince had noticed her in a crowd. But he hadn't. Theo was watching the beautiful and curvy brunette in front of Alex.

"He's watching you, not her," Jane said, trying to justify herself. They both knew who the prince had to be admiring.

A tap on the microphone in the front of the room was the only thing that could tear the gaze of the women around her from Prince Theo. Jacques stood at the podium, his signature premature white hair pulled back into a low ponytail and his shoulders erect.

"This is it." Alex squeezed Jane's hand as she felt the water she'd drunk earlier slosh around in her stomach. She'd been so nervous she didn't eat, and with the way the water was churning, she was glad she hadn't. Emmalee might have more than the best hair products money could buy running through her locks if Alex had eaten the granola bar Jane had offered.

"I think most of you have noticed our mystery judge join the panel," Jacques said.

The room was littered with nervous laughter as the females in the group were brought out of the "prince induced fog" many of them had fallen into, and recalled why they were there. Alex knew they were all feeling the same jitters as they waited for Jacques's announcement. Getting into the program they'd just completed was a once in a lifetime opportunity. Jacques only offered the course every five years. But the next step was just as important as the last. A one-month internship for only ten of them. Well, only nine of them since, unbeknownst to all but Jacques and the program directors, Jane, Alex's bodyguard, was guaranteed a spot just in case Alex made it that far. If Alex didn't make the top nine, Jane would drop out of the program and return to Litiana with Alex.

Making sure her bodyguard stayed in the program the entire time Alex did was the one requirement Mando had demanded before she left. If she hadn't agreed, he would have found a way to sabotage the whole thing. Alex had hated him for about ten seconds until she realized his motivation was love. Alex had secured a promise that he would pull no such strings for her and keep her identity a secret from everyone in the program, staff and participant alike. Mando had assured her that wouldn't be a problem and a compromise was reached.

But Alex couldn't help but wonder if she'd be a part of the ninety percent of the group that would leave the auditorium holding a certificate that could get them a decent photography position anywhere in the world. She couldn't think like that.

She had to believe, because only the last ten percent were still in the running for Alex's dream job.

Correction. It was more than a dream job. It was her dream, period. Joining Jacques's exploratory crew as they searched the world for sights as yet unseen and captured them on film was practically the only thing Alex could think about from the moment she learned about Jacques and what he did. Only the top of the ten interns would get that spot, and Alex wanted it more than anything.

"You may wonder why a prince has joined our panel," Jacques said, bringing Alex back to the present.

Several of the male members of the crowd nodded. The females didn't seem to care one way or the other as long as Prince Theo stayed in the room.

"Traditionally, the internship has been in a variety of places, mostly in the wild."

Alex thought back to the pictures she'd studied that the interns from five years before had taken of the icescapes in the arctic. There had been one that was a mass of all white, only the light of the sun had given the photo any kind of dimension. Alex didn't know what it was, but something about the picture called to her. She had to take one like it. She knew it was foolish to dream the internship would be in the same place. It never was. But as a part of Jacques's crew, she could get those kinds of photos one day.

"But we decided to do something a bit different this year. We will be focusing on portraits."

Alex felt her mouth drop open, but she quickly closed it. Portraits? It seemed so mundane for Jacques. Landscapes, architectural photos, candids of life, and even food art was more along the lines of what Jacques shot.

"And the Kane family has been kind enough to host us," Jacques said as he turned to Theo and waved a hand toward him with flourish.

Royal portraits? Alex swallowed a lump in her throat. She of all people knew how many hopeful individuals wanted the opportunity to capture a royal family. Those types of photographs would go down in history. But she could have done a royal portrait at home. As Alexandra Torre. She had plenty of brothers and their families to photograph. If this was the final test, what was the point of becoming Alex Turner?

Passing the test and making Jacques's team.

Alex nodded her head as she remembered her ultimate goal. So, her final stepping stone wouldn't be what she'd imagined, but who cared? When she became a member of Jacques's team, it wouldn't matter that she hadn't been a part of the group to shoot the slums of India or Big Ben.

This was just another hurdle to jump, and jump Alex would.

"The internship isn't the path for most of you in this room and that is nothing to be ashamed of."

Jacques continued on about how being a part of his program was an honor in itself. It was. But for Alex it wasn't enough.

He began to call out the names of graduates of the course and therefore the people who wouldn't be making the internship part of the program.

Lori was called and Emmalee grinned at her friend. Alex wasn't sure if it was a condolence smile or if she was smiling because her last name of Barclay had already passed and that meant Emmalee wasn't graduating yet. She was an intern.

Alex cursed that the last name she'd chosen was so late in the alphabet. It had seemed like a good idea, if not a slightly funny one, to use the name her brother Channing had when he'd hidden in the United States, but waiting as the H's and then the K's passed, Alex felt her insides twist a bit more with each name.

She noticed Cory Latham's name wasn't called. Like Emmalee, Cory being chosen wasn't a surprise to Alex. She tried to concentrate enough to see who else's names weren't called, but her mind hadn't been spared the wringing sensation her heart, stomach, and throat were also enduring.

Wait, *did* Theo know she was part of the program and was that why he was here? Did he come to mess things up since she'd denied his proposal?

Alex almost snorted out loud. The pressure must really be getting to her. Like one of the Valdorian princes would be torn up by her refusal enough to seek vengeance. She'd only ever been around Theo a handful of times in her life, the most recent was when she was eighteen and quite the snob, since she'd just started dating the guy she thought was the center of the universe. Prince Theo had probably thrown a party that he'd dodged a courtship with the brace-faced brat from Litiana.

Her thoughts had occupied her mind long enough that Jacques had gotten to r in the alphabet. Reyes, Smith, Thee.

Alex swallowed and placed her palms on her bouncing knees in an effort to calm them.

"Alfonso Victor," Jacques called.

Alex bit her lip in attempt to keep from crying out a victory shout. She'd made it. Jane squeezed a hand around Alex's upper arm and Alex beamed. She felt tears welling up in her eyes and felt silly. Alex Turner didn't cry. She covered her face with her hands and tried to surreptitiously wipe away the tears so that Jane wouldn't see them.

"And now we'd like to award the recipients of the internship," Jacques said.

Alex took a deep breath and sat up as straight as she could. There was no point in hiding from Theo anymore. She'd have to trust her disguise and hope that if he hadn't noticed her by now, he never would. Besides, he'd be a lot more likely to do it if she didn't act like all of the other girls in the program. Even if that meant fawning over the man that, in the few encounters she'd had with him, had an ego that matched his gorgeousness.

Two

Theo had almost done a double take when he saw her sitting in the fifth row of the auditorium. What was Alexandra Torre doing in a group full of photographer hopefuls? He remembered that her family and people close to her sometimes called her Alex but decided he would continue to call her Alexandra, even if it was just in his mind.

He felt his emotions range from anger to hurt and decided to suffocate them all, the way any good royal could, only allowing himself to feel a bit of annoyance toward the woman who'd run when he'd tried to begin to court her.

"We have quite the talented group this year," Patsy, one of the judges on the panel, whispered in Theo's ear.

Patsy had come on a bit strong in the past few days they'd spent together during the selection process of the interns and wasn't letting up. Theo's typical reaction would have been to slide a bit in his seat in the opposite direction from any woman like Patsy, but he was feeling a little reckless. Patsy was a beautiful, if not older, woman and Theo found himself reveling in the attention. He may or may not have spent a few moments after Patsy sidled up next to him looking for a reaction from a certain woman in the crowd.

Every other set of eyes was on him, except Alexandra's. Just Theo's luck.

Theo realized how unprofessionally he was treating the moment. Working out this arrangement with Jacques had been a nightmare and he was using the moment to get back at a woman who walked away from him. *Idiot.*

Theo's mother, Queen Marla, was a huge fan of Jacques's work and wanted no one else to take the thirtieth anniversary portrait of herself and Theo's father, as well as other commemorative family photos.

But Jacques didn't do portraits, even for a royal family.

So, Theo was sent to negotiate with the man and this was their happy medium. Theo and his family would host the interns, along with Jacques and Patsy, while the interns finished their final project. It was a month-long project that would culminate in Jacques and his students taking portraits alongside one another. Jacques taking photos would make his mother happy and the students taking them made Jacques happy. And before those portraits were taken, the chosen ten would spend the rest of the month catching candid photos of all the moments leading up to and including the huge anniversary ball the queen was throwing. Some of those photos would be kept for posterity's sake (his mother's words) and some for the occasional press release (his father's words). Jacques was happy, Theo's mother was happy, and in turn Theo, was happy. It was a win for all.

Until Alexandra.

He'd heard whisperings that the woman had left Litiana soon after his offer of courtship to her parents. It still rubbed him the wrong way that he'd had to use that course to pursue the woman he'd thought was perfect for him. But Litiana was stuck in their old ways, the only person to buck them being the country's fifth prince, Chandler. So, according to what he knew of Litiana's customs, if Theo wanted Alexandra, it meant he had to negotiate with her parents before attracting her interest.

Boy, had that blown up in his face. He still remembered the letter he'd received with Litiana's royal seal. Most of his correspondence was done over email, it was the twenty-first century after all. Even most royals had caught up. Except the Litians. The letter was full of flowery language that boiled down to one message. Alexandra wasn't interested.

But why had she ended up here? And why wasn't the rumor mill churning with this type of gossip? Theo cocked his head before realizing his thoughts were showing physically. He schooled his features and righted his head, turning his attention back to Jacques.

"Alfonso Victor," Jacques said as a head bobbed in the audience.

Theo didn't even try to hold back the small smile that formed on his face watching Alexandra all but spill out of her chair. So, she must have made the intern program.

What did that mean for him? The interns were coming to stay in his home. Granted, it was a castle so they wouldn't be tripping over one another, but still.

It meant nothing for him. She'd rejected him. A year and closer proximity wasn't going to change that.

Jacques completed the list of graduates and then began to call out the names of the interns.

"Emmalee Barclay," Jacques said.

A curvy, brunette stepped out from the row in front of where Alexandra sat. Had she been there the whole time? Theo's radar for beautiful women was renowned among his brothers and friends, but something had kept it from working that morning.

Theo was fooling himself if he thought the reason his radar wasn't working was something and not a certain someone.

Emmalee walked to the stage, as Jacques had directed her to do, but her eyes never strayed from Theo. She came to stand behind where he and Patsy sat, placing her hands on the back of

Theo's chair before leaning down to whisper into his ear. "Looks like we'll be working closely together for the next month. I look forward to it."

He felt a single finger trail up his suit clad bicep and over his shoulder before sitting up straighter and leaning away from the finger. Theo had come across far too many women like Emmalee and he knew his best bet was to keep his distance. Women like her had claws that clung and that was the last thing Theo needed.

Emmalee was directed to stand a bit further behind the judges, thank you Jacques, before the rest of the interns were called.

A woman named Nadine was called and she joined Emmalee, the former giving the latter a hug on arrival. A few more names were called before one that sounded familiar to Theo.

"Alex Turner," Jacques said.

Despite the androgynous name, Theo knew it was Alexandra before she stood. Turner had been the name her brother had used as an alias while he'd hid in the US. Was she doing the same thing?

Theo had never understood how Chandler had done it. His country, Valdoria, especially the media there, knew Theo's whereabouts at all times. Heck, even when he was in the US, he was spotted and photographed the moment he landed. Of course, the Litian royal family had done everything they could in the past ten years to fly below the radar and the Valdorians had done the opposite. His father had pushed them to be seen, saying that it improved their international relations. And while it did do that, it also brought uncomfortable situations like being named sexiest man of the year. Theo still cringed anytime he thought about the front cover of the popular magazine that his brothers had enlarged to life size and attached to Theo's personal office wall. Thankfully it wasn't a space he invited many people into, but somehow the poster had survived too many months. Theo really needed to take that down.

Somehow Chandler had hidden in plain sight in the US for years, and it looked like Alexandra was trying to do the same.

Theo watched as the stunning woman who'd caught his interest nearly seven years before walk to the stage. Sure, she'd dyed her hair blond, she wasn't wearing the makeup the Alexandra he'd known had, and those hideous glasses hid her gorgeous "where the green hills meet the blue ocean" eyes, but there was no way he wouldn't have recognized her. Why didn't everyone else?

"She could have at least tried to look presentable considering this is maybe one of the biggest moments of her life." Theo heard a female voice whisper.

He fought the urge to turn around and see who the voice belonged to, while also fighting the urge to stare at Alexandra who was now taking the steps onto the stage. He was doing a whole lot of fighting for a man sitting still.

It didn't matter who'd made the catty comment about Alexandra. She wasn't his to protect. *She had rejected him.* He wondered if he should get the phrase tattooed on the inside of his arm. At least that way he'd remember it.

"Jane Walker," Jacques finished and the hall erupted with applause for all of the interns and graduates.

The woman who had been sitting beside Alexandra came onto the stage, completing the group of ten behind him.

The graduates began to file out of the hall as Jacques and Patsy moved to congratulate the interns. Theo stood, realizing he should do the same.

He walked to a man who stood the farthest from Theo's seat and shook his hand.

"Congratulations, Cory," Theo said and the man responded with a smile and returned his handshake.

Theo was grateful for his diplomatic training that helped

him remember the names that had been called out, and match them with faces, even though his thoughts had been miles away most of the ceremony. His short-term memory was pretty fantastic. It was his long-term memory that often needed to be jogged by his assistant, Daniel.

As Theo moved along shaking hands and congratulating all the interns, he noticed that Alexandra, who had started somewhere in the middle of the group, had moved farther and farther down the line until she was the last person he would greet.

When he got to Jane, Alexandra began to move behind the woman as if she were going to go back to the start of the line and miss greeting Theo altogether.

Oh no, she didn't. If he was going to be grown-up and mature about this situation, so would she.

"Alex, wasn't it?" Theo said, even though he was still mid handshake with Jane.

Alexandra nodded and her cheeks became tinged with pink. She knew she'd been caught.

Jane quickly let go of Theo's hand and walked away, leaving no one to stand between Alexandra and Theo.

"I didn't want you to go before I could say congratulations. You do wonderful work," Theo said with a grin.

"Wait, my work? I thought, I didn't realize. So, you know...."

Theo allowed Alexandra to stutter a bit before responding. So maybe he wasn't being completely mature.

He had also let her go on a little longer because he'd been surprised by the Southern American accent that flowed from Alex's mouth. It was as good as any he'd ever heard, and if he'd only heard her voice, there was no way he would have recognized her.

"I'm assuming it was wonderful because all ten portfolios of the selected interns were extraordinary," Theo said, pulling his shoulders back and putting on what his mother called their regal stance.

"Oh, yes. Of course." Alexandra's cheeks had gone an even deeper shade of pink. "I should let you get back...." She left her thought unfinished and walked away as Emmalee and Nadine took her spot.

"You have to tell us all about Valdoria. I've heard it's beautiful," Emmalee said as she tucked some of her hair behind her ear.

"I can't believe we'll get to live there for a month. In the castle," Nadine said, earning her an elbow to the ribs from Emmalee.

Theo pretended not to notice the glare Emmalee gave her friend before saying, "We aren't just assuming we'll be staying in the castle. Jacques told us what we needed to pack for when he came to congratulate us."

"That makes sense since you'll be leaving tomorrow morning if I'm not mistaken," Theo said. It had been easy to maintain his regal stance during the conversation with these two women. He'd been told he came across as standoffish when he adopted the stance, and if he ever needed standoffishness while at the same time appearing diplomatic, this was the moment.

Emmalee took a step closer to Theo, invading his personal space, and he knew that was his cue.

"If you'll excuse me," Theo said before turning around to find anyone who could pull his attention away from the conversation he was escaping.

"We need to head out, sir," Daniel, Theo's assistant, said loud enough for the women to overhear.

"Yes. Thank you," Theo responded and Daniel knew exactly what the thanks was for. He'd been saving Theo from all kinds of situations in the past several years, but sadly this was the type they encountered most.

Daniel led Theo to Jacques.

"Accommodations are ready for you, Patsy, and the interns.

Also, we have a hall prepared for your instructional area," Theo said.

Jacques had informed him that since most of what his course covered had nothing to do with portraits, he would be taking some of the month getting the interns ready. Each intern would be assigned one type of family portrait while Jacques captured all. In between instructional sessions, Jacques, Patsy, and the interns would be invited to a few family and political events in order to shoot the candids Jacques had promised. There would also be a few interns who didn't need any type of instruction on portraits, Jacques had assured Theo, and they could take portraits of the busiest members of the family practically twenty-four/seven.

"Thank you. I know this situation isn't your ideal, but I am sure you will be happy with the end result. Who knows? Maybe your mother will prefer the interns' shots," Jacques joked.

That had been a silver lining in the negotiations. Theo had assumed Jacques was going to be an egotistical fool who couldn't see beyond his own talent, but instead he was surprisingly modest for one so gifted.

Theo saw Patsy closing in from one direction and Emmalee and Nadine from another.

"I'll see you soon," Theo said and Jacques laughed when he noticed the incoming women.

Daniel gently pushed through all three women and got Theo to the door unscathed.

That had been close.

After Theo, Daniel, and his two bodyguards got situated in the car that would take him to the airport, he groaned as a thought occurred to him. He'd just invited all three of those women into his home for a month.

Three

Packing was a cinch. Alex easily shoved her wardrobe and all personal items into one suitcase before taking her time to carefully place all of her camera equipment into a second suitcase. She hadn't bothered to decorate the walls of the dorm-like room she shared with Jane. At least she assumed it was dorm-like, since it was like the ones she'd seen on the American movies she'd binged watched before leaving Litiana. It was from those movies she'd adopted her style and even a bit of her attitude.

Moving to the US had been the first-time Alex had flown on a commercial airline; she'd told Mando a private plane was sure to raise red flags as to her true identity. And that was when she first found out the do's and dont's of flying. Like a person carrying more than two suitcases with them draws attention and that was the last thing she wanted. Thankfully, she had happened to pack light when she'd flown out to the intensive program so that hadn't been an issue for her.

As she finished her last-minute preparations, Alex made sure to fill her backpack with snacks and an empty bottle to fill with water later. Another rule she'd learned, that one the hard way, when a security agent had confiscated her water. But luckily, he was a nice guy and hadn't made a big deal of Alex's faux pas, so she was pretty sure no one around her even noticed.

The door to her room opened and closed quietly. Alex had wondered where Jane had gone. She hadn't come home until after Alex had gone to sleep the night before and was awake and out of their room before Alex arose. Alex knew Jane was avoiding her, as she should, considering the way she'd walked away from Alex the day before. Jane had been Alex's last buffer against Theo. And she'd left her high and dry.

"Are you packed?" Alex asked Jane, and she turned around in time to see the latter nod.

"What have you been up to?" Alex asked.

Jane shrugged. "Just some last-minute things before we leave."

"Hmm. So, your disappearance has nothing to do with the fact that you might think I'm a bit angry with you about yesterday?"

"Yesterday?" Jane was the picture of innocence.

Alex rolled her eyes. "How could you desert me like that? Isn't it your *job* to protect me?"

It was Jane's turn to give Alex the look she'd just received. "From the bad guys."

"Theo is a bad guy."

"*Prince* Theodore Bartholomew Kane III isn't a bad guy."

How could Jane be so sure? Because right now, Alex was sure of nothing. She'd been certain that leaving Litiana and all of her princess duties behind was the right decision until she was up close and personal with Theo yesterday. Her heart had raced and her cheeks flushed. She hated the reaction she had to the man. Attraction was the last thing she needed to feel for him. He was the opposite of her dream in every way.

"Would you care to explain why you felt you needed protecting from Theo, as you like to call him?" Jane continued.

"It's his name."

"Pretty sure I called him by his name. You called him the nickname adoring fans and members of his inner circle use."

Alex could see the teasing glint in Jane's eyes, but when jokes hit so close to the truth, it wasn't a laughing matter anymore.

"And why did you need protection?" Jane asked. "He doesn't know you're the woman who scorned him."

"I didn't scorn him," Alex muttered, trying to ignore the tiny bit of hurt she felt that Theo hadn't recognized her. It was ridiculous because if he had, everything would have fallen to ruins, but some tiny sadistic part of herself wanted him to know her and care that she hadn't gone through with the attempted arrangement. She was a moron.

"So, this is according to what *you've* told me, he doesn't recognize you as the woman who scorned him and you did nothing to deserve his wrath. Either way, you wouldn't need protecting. Unless it isn't *his* feelings you're worried about."

Alex shook her head, willing the conversation to stop, no longer concerned that Jane deserted her and only concerned with how she was supposed to survive the next month when she could barely manage a two-minute conversation with the man who was hosting them.

She took a deep breath.

By being a dang professional. This was her career. If she couldn't woman up in this situation, she'd be a lost cause anywhere.

"What time does our flight leave?" Alex asked.

Jane grinned, knowing she'd won this round. "The van to the airport leaves in an hour."

Alex nodded and ignored Jane humming happily and putting her clothes in a suitcase of her own. When Mando had suggested Jane as Alex's guard, Alex had jumped at the opportunity. Having a woman guard was much less suspect than a male in this situation. It was easy to pretend the two became best friends when they were placed in a room together. They were going to create a fake friendship that had started before the course, but since Jacques knew Jane was in the program because of Mando's influence, any past relationship of Jane's, fake or otherwise, would be under scrutiny.

So, their back story was that Jane had attended a photography program at some fancy college right before the course. And Alex was a small-town girl who stayed home to hone her skill. It wasn't far from the truth, except Jane had gone to college to study how to kill a man in a hundred ways before he even noticed she'd entered the room. Okay, maybe that wasn't her exact course of study, but it was something like that. And Alex had lived in her castle on the hill attending parties and being dumped by the guy who had promised to treasure her. Not that she was still bitter or anything.

Alex shifted her attention to the room she stood in, no longer wanting to think about home or him. There was nothing left for her to do, so she lay back onto the mattress, one of the few things she was leaving behind, and closed her eyes.

Four flights and two car rides later, the van transporting the interns pulled into the circular drive in front of the royal dwelling in Valdoria. The white stone castle loomed in front of them and, though she'd seen castles, including this one in particular, many times before, even Alex was impressed.

"This is incredible," Nadia said under her breath.

Although Alex's childhood home was also a castle, it was almost unfair to her poor home to put it in the same category as the one the Valdorians boasted. Theo's father, Theodore Bartholomew Kane II, besides being a king was a showman, and had added to the family home extensively during his lifetime. In the five years since Alex had last visited, she swore the size of it had doubled. Well, maybe that was a stretch, but still, it was huge.

And the actual building was only part of what held the group in awe. Rolling green hills surrounded the castle and perfectly trimmed hedges lined the drive filled with purple flowers in full bloom. Marble statues of ancient Valdorian guards stood on either side of every marble step leading up to the castle doors that looked like they were made from pure gold. King Theodore had spared no expense.

All signs of jet lag that had plagued the group moments before disappeared.

A doorman opened the passenger door of the vehicle as soon as it came to a complete stop and the interns piled out as quickly as humanly possible.

"We can take them all to the assigned rooms," the doorman said, motioning to a waiting attendant with a rolling luggage rack, stopping Jacques from going to the rear of the van to get the suitcases on his own.

"Thank you," Jacques said. Even he seemed a little out of his element.

The enormous gold doors opened, and out walked Queen Marla herself. Alex fell to the back of the group, doing her best to keep from being seen. Theo might have skimmed past her face in the crowd, but if anyone could pick her out, it would be the Valdorian queen. She prided herself on never forgetting a face. Hopefully, Alex's face had always been too young or too made up for Queen Marla to remember.

"Jacques," Queen Marla said as she seemed to float toward the man, putting her hands on his shoulders and brushing his cheeks with a kiss each. What was it with queens and grace? Alex's mother moved in the same way Queen Marla did, and Alex had no idea how they accomplished the task. Another reason it was a good thing that Alex had denied Theo's parents' proposal. Alex would never have that sort of grace.

The man's face flamed a bright red and Alex grinned, grateful she was hiding her head behind Cory's rather large one. Jacques would not appreciate being laughed at. But it was hilarious to see the man who in the year she'd known him had never lost his composure blush over one tiny gesture.

"We are so grateful you're here. That you all are here." Queen Marla said the second sentence as she turned to the group standing to the side of where she and Jacques stood.

Alex ducked quickly and wondered how she was going to manage this for her entire internship. She was sure to have to have contact with the queen at some point. She was living in her home. But then again, the castle was larger than many hotels and maybe she could fly under the radar. At least for a while, until she came up with a better plan than cowering behind Cory.

"I'm sure you all want to freshen up a bit and could probably use a good nap," Queen Marla said.

"We're here to work, madam," Jacques said, and Alex heard a quiet groan erupt from Cory. "They can sleep tonight."

"Wonderful. But you'll want to see your rooms?" the queen asked.

Jacques nodded.

"Victor will show you to your rooms and then we'll meet for tea in, let's say, one hour?"

Jacques nodded again before the queen swept away and back into the castle.

Alex wiped her sweaty palms on her jeans as she straightened, hoping no one had noticed her attempt to hide, and Victor, the doorman, led them into the castle.

Maybe, just maybe, God would show her some mercy and she'd be able to conceal her identity a bit longer. She just had to get the job with Jacques as Alex Turner. Then the whole world could know who she was. But she had to get this job on her own merit. The Torre name had given her everything, and she was grateful for all she had. But she wanted this to be her win, and it would be tainted if anyone noticed who she really was.

The group oohed and aahed as they entered through the gold doors and into the castle. Alex tried to concentrate on the decor and not the very real possibility of her dream's impending doom. The inside was beautiful, but it seemed the king had gone for less of a "wow factor" indoors. Much of what Alex saw was like the home she grew up in. Busts of famous Valdorians, paintings of bygone royal families, and the art of the best and brightest in their country. Large, gleaming, gray stone tiles covered the ground and a twenty-foot-wide white staircase made from the same marble as the stairs outside led up to the next floor.

"You'll be staying on the fourth floor," Victor said as he led them away from the stairs and toward a set of wooden double doors. He pushed a button and the doors slid aside, revealing an elevator. It was the same perfect mix of old and new that Alex remembered from past visits to the Valdorian castle.

She realized everyone had gasped at the opening of the elevator doors, and she did the same quietly since her gasp was a bit belated.

After riding on the elevator, the group walked down a carpeted hall that Alex assumed the queen picked since it was blush pink. Each of the doors had a sign on them that welcomed a guest.

Jacques's was the first room and he reminded everyone to be ready in fifty minutes.

"This room!" Emmalee gushed as soon as she opened her door and then slammed it shut behind her.

They continued down the hall and someone left the group at each door until they came to the last room where Alex saw her name.

There were now only forty minutes until they were to meet back with the queen, and the last thing Alex wanted to do was make a late entrance. The only way her dream might survive was to fly under the radar and hope that her disguise held up. She tore through her bags which had been left next to the four-poster bed in the room and threw all of her t-shirts and jeans onto said bed. Unless she wanted to stick out like a sore thumb, she needed the one dress she had kept in case of an emergency.

She kicked off her Converses and tore off her socks, moaning as her toes sunk into the lush carpet. She'd forgotten what a luxury good flooring was. She couldn't wait to try the bed, but there was no time.

Thankfully her room had an ensuite bath and she took a quick shower to wash off all of the travel grime, rebraided her hair, and threw on the dress. Not wearing makeup had its perks.

She had a pair of flats that she'd kept for the same reasons as the dress and put them on before hurrying out the door with a few minutes to spare. Rich, Joe, Taylor, Cory, Jacques, and Jane stood by the elevator as Alex walked down the long hall. She would need a few extra minutes everyday thanks to where her room was positioned. She wondered if her placement had been on purpose but laughed at the thought. Her brother, Mando, had always teased Alex for her suspicious nature.

"What are you laughing at?" Jane whispered when Alex joined the group.

"Myself," Alex said, and Jane raised an eyebrow but didn't have a chance to say anything else.

"I think we should head on down," Jacques said to the group. "Patsy can join us with the stragglers."

Alex heard her stomach growl and hoped that the food portion of the tea would be waiting when they got downstairs. She could use a dozen or so finger sandwiches.

A few doors slammed as the group stepped into the elevator and Patsy, Nadine, Emmalee, and Miles ran toward them as Jacques held the doors open. Patsy had been Jacques's right hand woman for most of the course and, like her boss, had always seemed the epitome of composure. It appeared the prospect of tea with a queen ruffled even the most coifed of feathers.

Victor somehow appeared as the elevator opened on the first floor and guided them out of the main foyer down one of the several hallways that left the room.

The left side of the corridor they walked through ran along the front of the house, and floor to ceiling windows let in natural light that had Alex's photographer heart singing. She knew she had to get at least one of her candids in this hall.

Victor knocked on a set of double doors that looked like the elevator entry and stepped aside as they opened.

Alex stood back and allowed the group to move into the room in front of her. She saw every female head, including Jane's, bob to four different areas of the room. If that wasn't a sign that all four Valdorian princes were present, Alex didn't know what was.

She hoped her fresh face, glasses, and blond hair would do their job with people she'd already met. Theo would have been the easiest to trick since he had always been busy with his own thing and had his eyes on other girls, namely his dates, most every time her family had come to visit.

She wasn't being completely fair. He'd actually spent quite a bit of time with her on her last visit to Valdoria, but Alex had spent most of her time talking about her amazing (gag her) boyfriend, Pedro, and being a downright bore.

Out of habit, she'd ducked behind Cory again and realized she hadn't come up with a better plan for hiding her identity. Racking her brain for some way of preserving her disguise for as long as possible, Alex risked a peek around Cory's head (he was proving to be quite the good hiding spot) to assess the situation when she saw the queen looking directly at her.

Alex's breath caught in her throat and she knew the jig was up.

But then the queen's eyes moved on without a hint of recognition in them.

Alex glanced a little to her left and met Elliot's eyes. He was the youngest Valdorain prince, and since they were the same age, Elliot was the one Alex had spent the most time with. She waited for him to greet her by name and ask why she'd gone blond but was instead met by the signature smirk he gave every girl. One that he hadn't used on Alex since they were fourteen.

This seemed too good to be true. Granted, the Kanes weren't the closest of family friends, but Alex must have visited them or vice versa at least four times in her life. But then again, there were many who ran in the same social circle as the Kanes. The Torres were a bit different. They hadn't ever entertained much, and did so even less after her sister, Lizzie, had passed.

Maybe Alex hadn't made any sort of lasting impression on the group. That just proved how silly the whole courtship thing had been. If they didn't recognize her even after that, it had to signify the attempted arrangement meant even less to them than it did to her. Which, depending on how you looked at it, could be depressing, but in Alex's situation she couldn't be more thrilled.

Theo, Queen Marla, and Elliot down. This was happening. She was hiding in plain sight and felt a rush of adrenaline. It wasn't a wonder her brother Chandler had done the same for years. She could get used to this kind of high.

Alex became a bit bolder and stepped out fully from behind Cory as Queen Marla made introductions. Alex scanned the room and locked eyes with King Theodore. She wasn't surprised at the lack of recognition there. Prince Tristan winked and Prince Sebastian or Seb, as they all called him, grinned at her when they were introduced. But like Elliot's smirk, that meant nothing. She'd figured out where Theo was standing based on where the most female heads had turned and avoided looking in that direction. Even if he didn't know who she was, she didn't exactly appreciate the reaction her body had to the man.

She knew it was strictly physical attraction, what woman wasn't attracted to Prince Theo, and it was something she'd dealt with since her school girl crush on him when she was eight, the first time the Kanes visited the Torreses in Litiana. She'd been devastated when Theo introduced himself to Lizzie first and then kissed her hand, none of which he'd done for Alex. Not that she'd begrudge Lizzie anything now, but eight-year-old Alex didn't know any better. Maybe that was part of the reason she'd turned down Theo's proposal of courtship. To get back at the boy who'd ignored her. But then again, it wasn't Theo who'd asked. His parents talked to her parents. It didn't get more romantic than that. Not.

"And this lovely woman is Theo's girlfriend...." Queen Marla said.

Theo had a girlfriend? Alex watched as Emmalee, Nadine, and Patsy's heads snapped from the Queen to Theo. Judging by the reactions, at least Alex wasn't alone in her shock.

"Elise," Queen Marla finished.

Alex felt all of the air whoosh out of her lungs and gasped to take another breath. She felt Jane grip her arm as Alex's eyes collided with the one woman who'd hurt her more than any other.

Elise, Alex's ex-best friend, stood smiling smugly as she walked to Theo and placed her hand possessively on his bicep.

Theo and Elise? How was that even possible? The last she'd seen, Elise had been on the arm of the one man who'd hurt Alex more than any other - Pedro, her boyfriend of three years. It didn't make any sense.

But judging by the grip Elise had on Theo, she'd moved on.

Some part of Alex's mind told her to get out of sight. It was one thing to be able to fool strangers and people she'd vaca-tioned with a few times, but Elise was different. They'd spent as many hours together as they could from the time Alex was eighteen until Elise broke her heart when she was twenty-one.

Just as Alex was about to step behind Cory again to regroup and hopefully come up with a better plan than some eyeglasses, Elise's gaze rested on her. And just as quickly as Elise's attention came, it went. No recognition crossed her features. How could Elise not know her? The person she'd befriended and then betrayed.

And then it hit Alex like a ton of bricks. Alex had been a means to an end, Pedro, for Elise. Elise looked at her like a rung on a ladder. You didn't really look into the face of one you knew you'd crush on your way to the top.

Elise had caused all sorts of emotions in Alex before - anger, hurt, jealousy - but this emotion was new. Alex felt hatred bubble up in her chest and didn't even attempt to put a lid on it.

Four

Theo glanced around the room and wondered when Alexandra's charade would be discovered. Surely someone in his family would greet her by name.

But as time went on, no one did. His brothers gave their trademark flirtatious looks to Alexandra, and Theo felt something between amusement and annoyance at them. The famous Torre eyes were hidden by a tiny piece of glass. Glass. A see-through object.

He felt a tug on his arm and looked down at Elise. He'd extended a vague invite for her to come and stay at the castle anytime. He'd been a bit surprised to find that she'd decided to come early for the thirtieth anniversary celebrations, and at the same time the interns were visiting, but was happy to have her nonetheless. He didn't appreciate the attraction he had felt toward Alexandra, which had to be purely his appreciation of a beautiful woman. But if anything would cure that, it would be Elise.

They hadn't been dating for long, his mother had set them up, but she seemed like a nice girl. He may have been against the way the Litians arranged marriages, but for some reason it felt okay when his mother had invited Elise and her family to dinner as an obvious way to introduce her to Theo. Maybe it was because they both had a say in whether they were interested or not. And it was only a date that came next, not a courtship, which felt way too eighteen-hundreds. Wait, Elise was from Litiana. She'd *have* to recognize Alexandra.

Theo looked down and smiled at Elise as his mother introduced her, and then he watched as Elise gave a polite smile to every intern in the room. He was a bit annoyed when his mother had introduced Elise as his girlfriend since they were only dating and weren't a couple. But he did like the way Elise handled social situations with grace. As his mother liked to point out, it was the perfect trait for a queen. Not that Theo was close to bestowing a ring or crown on Elise; they were barely even dating.

His thoughts were torn from Elise as he watched Alexandra sway, looking almost like she might faint, and Theo felt himself lurch forward. Before he could actually run toward Alexandra, her friend Jane caught her, and Theo covered his lurch with a cough.

Alexandra seemed to steady, and Theo kicked himself for his reaction. But he was just doing his duty as a gentleman. He would have done the same for any woman in the room. Right?

He turned his attention back to the woman he should have been focusing on all along and watched as Elise made eye contact with Alexandra, then moved on without any sign of knowing the princess. Seriously?

Even if Elise hadn't recognized Alexandra, judging by the squint of Alexandra's eyes, they definitely knew each other. And if looks could kill, Elise would have been fried on the spot. Theo put his arm around Elise and pulled her close to him, sending Alexandra a searing glare of his own. But it went unnoticed as Alexandra wouldn't tear her eyes away from Elise.

Theo made a mental note to watch out for Elise and then

found a place for the two of them to sit once his mother finished introducing the interns.

Sandwiches, cakes, and tea were served as Jacques and his mother took turns letting the interns know the rules for their stay. His father had somehow managed to slip away, and Theo wished he could do the same. Elise might have the right idea as Theo saw out of the side of his eye that she was scrolling through something or other on her phone.

But in case his mother looked his way, Theo stayed away from his phone. This project was partially Theo's doing, and he had to at least appear invested. But it was proving to be quite the challenge as his mother and Jacques went on and on. In his attempt to keep the boredom at bay, he had, without realizing, begun searching for Alexandra, even as he worried that she might have a vendetta against Elise. Maybe he just wanted to see if the look of anger was still there? Fat chance.

"And all cameras will be turned in at the end of each day," Jacques said before his mother added, "And all downloading of photos will be done by Jacques or Patsy on the castle computers."

Theo knew that one of the rules for attending the internship was that no one could bring a laptop of their own and all phones were confiscated and replaced with ancient ones that didn't offer internet access. Theo didn't even know those existed anymore. Even though they'd done an extensive background check on each intern, no one wanted to take the chance that a non-approved photo would slip through the cracks and onto a front page. King Theodore appreciated media coverage, but it was always on his terms.

A thought occurred to Theo. Alexandra had been through the background check and no one had found anything odd. So her past must have been forged. Could anyone else have done the same?

Theo shook those thoughts out of his mind. Anyone with

bad intent would have had to have faked their identities and gotten into the program even before Theo had talked to Jacques about hiring him for the anniversary photos. No one, not even Theo, knew that the internship for this class would be in Valdoria at the beginning of the course.

Alexandra was only hiding in the program, well who knew why the Torreses chose to hide, for some personal reason he was sure. Nothing to do with him nor his family. Besides, Alexandra had a government to do her bidding. Forging an identity, if they wanted it, wouldn't be too hard for a royal. Hiding with said identity would be the hard part. But somehow Alexandra was managing it. Even in front of his family, people who knew her. It still bugged him that no one saw through her but him.

Theo looked over at Alexandra again and this time her focus was on the tall guy with the big head she kept hiding behind, Cory. At least she was no longer shooting daggers at Elise.

"Prince Theo." He recognized Emmalee's voice and realized she'd taken the seat on the other side of him where Elise wasn't seated.

"Emmalee," he said and then realized he shouldn't have used her name with the way she was beaming.

"I just wanted to thank you again for inviting us into your home," Emmalee said, and Theo felt his whole-body tense as Emmalee placed a hand on Theo's arm, and began stroking it. He pulled it away quickly. He was used to women coming out of their way to talk to him and more, but he hoped it wouldn't bother Elise. She had only spent time with him on dates or in small group settings. She hadn't been exposed to this side of his life.

"Everyone who knows him as well as *I* do knows he's a wonderful man with a generous spirit," Elise said, putting her phone down and popping her head out from around Theo's shoulder.

Emmalee's eyes narrowed and then went wide at Elise's

words. The declaration that the wonderful man had been claimed by Elise wasn't lost on Emmalee.

"He is," Emmalee replied.

"And we're all grateful to have you all with us," Elise said kindly, but showing the distinction between family and interns. This woman was a pro.

"Likewise," Emmalee said before vacating her seat.

He'd done enough pining over Alexandra, Elise had proven she was the woman for him. Theo turned his body toward Elise and said, "I hope you don't mind that we could have a camera flashing in our faces at any moment."

"Not in the least," Elise responded with a smile. "Besides, it will be nice to have some of our moments captured forever, won't it?"

And she found a bright side even in this. She was passing tests Theo didn't even know he was giving. He felt much more confident facing Alexandra, he meant, the interns, with Elise by his side.

Theo smiled back. "It will."

Five

Alex had a night to sleep on her anger, but she was still stewing in it when she awoke the next morning. Better to feel anger than like the fool that Elise had made her feel in the past.

She kicked off her covers and looked down at the ratty t-shirt and pajama shorts she'd started sleeping in as soon as she'd left her family home. It had felt right in her dorm room in Georgia, but being back in a castle was messing with Alex's head. Was she still the photography student she'd worked so hard to become, or now that she was back in a castle did she go back to being the princess her mother had raised her to be? There was nothing wrong with either person, and that fact didn't help her confusion in the least.

The photography student side of her had earned a spot in the most prestigious course on the planet and risen to the top of that group. Alex Turner, without the clout of the Torre name, had done that. Of course, growing up, she'd always been told her work was good. Who was going to tell the princess she stunk at her little hobby? But getting praise about her work purely because of her work? It was unlike anything Alex had ever experienced.

But that being said, despite the word pampered often being attached to her title, Alexandra had been anything but. She'd worked hard alongside her mother, even going into the soup kitchens to help serve and changing a diaper or two in an orphanage. Although it caused some waves among the upper class, the people she served and her parents were proud of her.

So, who was she supposed to be now?

Neither.

She was a photography intern now, more than just a student of Jacques's, vying for a job that any photographer in the world would sacrifice their favorite camera to get. And thanks to no one recognizing her, including her best friend of many years, she was still in the running without the prestige or taint the Torre name would give her.

Perhaps Alex should be thanking Elise for caring so little? Nope. Maybe princesses were supposed to be forgiving, but forgiving Elise was asking too much. However, even if she didn't forgive her, she had to get the hate she was feeling out of her system. She wouldn't do her job well if she was blinded by an emotion. She'd worked too dang hard to let Elise get in her way.

A shower. That's what she needed. It would cure a whole lot.

Alex climbed out of bed and walked toward the bathroom when a light knock sounded on her door. She looked down at her outfit and knew that her mother would have a fit if Alex allowed anyone to see her like that, but Queen Elizabeth wasn't there.

"Come in," Alex said.

The door opened and instead of a person, a rolling rack of clothes entered her room. Alex eyed the clothes and caught glimpses of a tiny red-headed woman when the clothes swayed just right. Then she heard the slamming of the door. How was someone so small navigating a rack that large with such ease?

"Alex Turner, correct?" The woman's accent was obviously Valdorian.

"That's me," Alex said, using her carefully honed American southern accent.

"Jewel Huber," the redhead said with her hand outstretched. The woman was almost a head shorter than Alex's five-foot-seven and was maybe the most delicate female Alex had ever seen. And that was saying a lot considering Alex had spent her formative years with royals and other noble people.

Alex took Jewel's hand and her eyes widened at the strength of the tiny woman's grip.

"Jacques told me you'd need some better outfit choices for your new assignment," Jewel said, leaving a bewildered Alex standing as Jewel left to open the door and let in a breakfast cart.

Had someone knocked on the door? Alex hadn't even heard it.

Alex read a book when she was six about a fairy who had come to live with a princess. This situation felt oddly like that book.

"Assignment?" Alex asked.

"You'll hear all about it in class this morning. You do know you have class with Jacques in an hour?"

Alex nodded. Jacques had told them that much the night before. She had been a bit suspicious when he didn't say anything about meeting daily at the same time for said class. Was this where the assignment came in?

"Is everyone getting new wardrobes?" Alex asked.

"Do you want the truth or a sugar-coated lie?" Jewel asked.

Alex tilted her head, wondering if she'd heard correctly, but the raised "no-patience" eyebrows on Jewel's face told her she had.

"The truth," Alex said.

"According to Patsy, and I quote, 'her wardrobe is atrocious and not up to the task Jacques has assigned her'."

Alex wasn't surprised by Patsy's declaration; her outfit choices weren't meant to impress. But what did catch her attention was the second part of what Jewel had said. "Do you know the task I've been assigned?" Alex asked.

Jewel nodded.

"But you won't be telling me?"

"You are just as smart as you look," Jewel said as she whipped down half a dozen dresses and held them up to Alex. "These are perfect." She took the dresses and walked toward the closet on the other side of Alex's room and hung them.

"I can get my own clothing," Alex said as she followed Jewel.

"I'm sure you can. But isn't it much more fun to let me do it. Besides, it's my job," Jewel called over her shoulder.

"And you don't trust me to choose my own clothing?"

"You hit the nail on the head. That's something you Americans say, right?" Jewel asked.

Alex wasn't sure whether to giggle or be offended so she went with a nod. "Do you work for Jacques?"

Jewel shook her head as she walked back to the rack and pulled off an armload of pants and tops.

"Nope. For the Kane family."

Alex's eyes went wide. There was only one person in a royal home that handed out clothing.

"You're the royal tailor?" Alex asked, her voice going up a notch. There was no way her own family's royal tailor would have deigned to dress someone as simple as Alex was pretending to be. Despite the average title, royal tailors worked their entire lives to achieve a position of such prestige. Alex had never met one so approachable or so young.

"Yes," Jewel said, and Alex waited for her to go on with how she'd been coerced into doing this job, but she didn't. She seemed genuinely happy to be helping Alex.

Jewel walked the armload of clothes to Alex's closet. Where was her assistant?

"Do you need some help?" Alex asked as she walked into the closet to join Jewel.

"Nope. Prefer to work alone," she said, each word a bit strained as she pushed on to her tip toes to reach the top rod in the closet.

"Should I try them on?" Alex asked.

"No need. I've got an eye, or so they say," Jewel said before depositing the last pair of pants and turning to Alex. "Each pair of pants is next to its corresponding top. Please wear them as outfits until I can get back to teach you about matching things."

Alex fought hard to keep from laughing out loud. Little did Jewel know Alex had been having those same types of lessons all her life and had purposely gone against them all in her quest to stay hidden as Alex Turner. Wait, would this clothing be like a neon sign that she wasn't Alex Turner?

She shook her head. If no one had noticed her up until this point, a few outfit changes wouldn't make a difference.

"Sorry, they've got me on a tight schedule. Apparently, a guy named Rich has worn the same pair of jeans for six weeks straight?" Jewel said, her pixie-like face screwed up in a look of disgust.

She didn't wait for Alex to answer and rushed to the clothing rack, pushing it toward the door.

"I think I like you, Alex Turner," she said before opening the door and whooshing out of the room.

Alex wasn't positive, but she thought she liked Jewel too.

Jane's mouth quirked into a half frown/half smirk when she met Alex in the hallway.

"Channeling some of that inner Torre?" Jane asked, eyeing Alex's new ensemble as they walked toward the elevator. Alex had paired one of the simpler pair of black trousers with a navy and white striped silk shirt.

Alex frowned. "Shh! What if someone heard you?"

"Would it really be the end of the world for your true identity to come out?" Jane asked.

"Yes. It would," Alex said in voice that she hoped left no room for interpretation.

"Fine." Jane sulked.

Alex wondered where Jane's attitude was coming from. Of all people, Jane should be glad the world thought of her as Alex Turner. A photography intern was a whole lot easier to guard than a princess. She thought about asking Jane what her issue was, but between encountering Elise and getting a whole new wardrobe, Alex felt pretty emotionally worn. She'd deal with Jane's issues another day or just wait for them to disappear; they sometimes did that.

"So, what's up with these new assignments?" Alex asked.

"New assignments?" Jane parroted as they got off the elevator on the second floor and walked toward the princes' old schoolroom that had been transformed into the instruction room Jacques would use.

"Yeah. Jewel mentioned we'd be getting them."

"Jewel as in the royal ones?"

"Oh no. I met the Valdorian royal tailor this morning."

"Ah. Hence the new wardrobe."

At the second mention of her wardrobe, Alex noticed what Jane was wearing.

"Wait, why is what you wear okay and what I wore isn't?" Alex asked, giving Jane a once over. Jane wore her standard black fitted pants with a black button-up and black boots.

"Maybe because I have style."

"Black isn't a style," Alex retorted, feeling quite annoyed. Jane just grinned knowing she had no comeback, but she'd still somehow won.

The women walked into Jacques's classroom and Alex stopped in the doorway. Jane glanced back at her and then pulled on her arm, leading her to one of the few open seats. The room held one large, dark, wooden table that looked old enough to have seated many Kane royals over the generations and would sell for more than most luxury cars. The room was decorated with adorable portraits and paintings of the Valdorian princes through the years, all hanging above a chalkboard on one wall and a white board along another. The last two walls were floor to ceiling windows. With that kind of natural light it wasn't a surprise Jacques had chosen this room to instruct his interns.

But it was none of those things that stopped Alex in her tracks. Posted on the whiteboard were photo after photo, many of which Alex had taken. Seeing her work in a setting like this was eerie. This room was too much like her old schoolroom, the hall she'd walked down too much like the ones she'd run through all of her life. Parts of her she had worked so hard to keep apart were colliding.

She drew in a deep breath and realized she'd have to suck it up. Elise, the castle, the new wardrobe, Theo, they were all a part of her new normal. At least for now. She could deal with it. For now.

Taylor ran through the door and Jacques looked at him with narrowed eyes before he began to speak. Right on time was five minutes late in Jacques's book.

"Have you noticed anything about the photos we have up?" he asked.

"They're all portraits and candids," Emmalee answered, sounding entirely too confident.

Jacques nodded.

"I know we didn't cover the how-tos of portraiture for very long during my course, but for some of you, judging from your photos, that time was all you needed. On the other hand, we spent plenty of time on how to get the best candid shot. You can see that by considering the progression from the shots you took when you entered the course to those in your final portfolios." Jacques pointed out Taylor's first candid shot of Nadine that had the lighting and lines all wrong to his latest offering of a little boy playing on the beach which looked like it could be on the cover of any photography book.

"So, most of our class time here will be spent learning more about how to capture the best portrait shots. They must be perfect for the royal family. And although I'll be taking photos along with you, I would love to include a shot or two from my future employee in the package of photos I present to the Kanes."

Alex felt her heart skitter at those words. *Future employee.*

"With the queen, we decided," Jacques motioned between himself and Patsy, "that the royal family would appreciate candid shots of the entire month. The events of this month lead up to a major celebration that the Kanes will be holding for their thirtieth wedding anniversary. The easiest way to do this will be to assign an intern who already understands portrait photography to each of the members of the royal family who will be appearing in public the most. Then those who need more instructional time with me will be assigned family candids and shots of the members of the family who aren't assigned a specific intern."

So, these were the assignments. Alex knew she needed one of those personal assignments. More instructional time meant bottom of the totem pole. Although they could maybe learn to be better portrait takers over time, a month wasn't very long, and the likelihood of rising from the bottom wasn't high. The top assignments meant they were closer to the job. Alex wanted to be as close as she could be.

"I won't beat around the bush. There are three top assignments. The interns assigned these jobs will be following their designated royal family member practically twenty-four hours a day and, therefore, will have no more instructional time with me. But rest assured, I feel completely confident in the three of these interns' abilities to take a portrait worthy of a queen. Literally."

No one laughed at Jacques's joke, and as Alex scanned the nervous faces in the room, she realized the significance of these assignments were hitting all of them at once.

She remembered back to when she first started Jacques's course and he'd done a similar thing. He'd collected all of her colleagues into three groups and wasn't shy about saying which ones had come into the course with the top portfolios and which group was full of the hopefuls that had gotten in by the skin of their teeth. As she compared those groups with the people sitting next to her, Alex realized the only person that made the position of intern from that bottom group was Jane, and Alex knew she wasn't here on her own merits. Jane could take a decent picture, part of why she had been assigned as Alex's bodyguard during the course, but she had no passion for it. Alex was, embarrassingly, a part of the middle group. She and Taylor were the only ones that had risen from there and, she wasn't going to fool herself, she knew it had taken almost the full-year course for Alex to prove herself. She didn't have a year this time. She needed a top spot. Even if Jacques didn't come right out and say it, anything other than a top spot meant the death of her dream.

"Cory will be shadowing the king," Jacques began.

Alex nodded, even as disappointment coursed through her. Although he was her competition, she was a fan of Cory's work. The way he captured moments made one feel like they'd walked back into that moment in time. Cory's work evoked feeling whether he shot a tree in the midst of many or a wave crashing to shore.

"Emmalee, the queen."

Alex felt her heart lodge in her throat. She should have seen

Emmalee's assignment coming, but she'd hoped for a different outcome. Cory and Rich had been the top two students during the entire course, leaving the number three spot up for grabs. In the end, it was Emmalee and Alex who were neck and neck as they vied for the spot, and it looked like Emmalee had won.

She wiped her hands on her new pants. So, although there was technically still one spot open, everyone knew it was Rich's. But Alex couldn't help but hope.

"The king and queen will both be busy in the days before their thirtieth anniversary, and it is an even bigger ordeal for the king, as his wedding was the second anniversary of his coronation," Jacques went on.

Who cares? Alex just needed him to give out the last assignment. She avoided the eyes of everyone else in the room. She knew Rich would have a knowing smile on his face, and the rest of the interns would be looking to him. The outcome was sure in all of their minds. But Alex's hope could stay alive if she kept her eyes solely on Jacques.

"And the third assignment goes to Alex," Jacques said.

She heard a gasp to her left and wondered if it came from Rich, but she had to keep looking straight ahead because if she didn't, she knew everyone would hate her. The smile that had spread across her face was huge. There was no room in her joy to feel bad for Rich. She'd done it.

She'd never been so glad to read a situation all wrong. If she'd gotten the spot over Rich, who knew if Cory was still at the top? Maybe she'd elbowed her way to the top without even knowing? A girl could dream.

"You'll be capturing candid shots of...." Jacques began.

Wait. Alex hadn't thought that far. The king and queen needing a personal photographer made sense, but why would there be a need for a third intern that would photograph someone twenty-four/seven? It had to be one of the princes and why would one of the princes need to be trailed more than the others? A similar feeling to the one she got the time she ate cold pizza with milk congealed in her stomach. She knew, but didn't want to admit who she was going to have to spend day in and day out with. Maybe there was a chance they'd want her to tail Elliot? There was absolutely no reason for her to be Elliot's personal photographer other than the pure fact that she couldn't handle it if her assignment was....

"Crown Prince Theo."

Six

ven before she walked into his office, Theo knew who his photographer would be. Call it a gut feeling or more like a sinking gut, he just knew.

What he didn't expect was her new look. She'd kept the blond braid and fake glasses, but the clothes she wore were a blatant reminder that she was Princess Alexandra, the woman who'd run rather than date him.

But he had to push all of that aside since they were both pretending she wasn't the princess. Theo wasn't sure when he'd become a player in her charade, and he wasn't sure he liked it, but here he was playing her game. He guessed he wouldn't reveal her without knowing her reasons for hiding. He'd learned long ago it was best to keep his hand close to his chest until he had all the facts, and life was nicer when you made the best of every situation. He'd be relying on both of those lessons in the next few weeks.

"I hear we'll be spending quite a bit of time together," Theo said, trying not to smile when he saw her bite her lip. Maybe it would be just as hard for her to spend time with him as it was for him to with her. Unlikely.

"It will be an honor to capture your fine moments,"

Alexandra said. It was evident in her demeanor that she thought the whole "capturing every moment of the next month of Theo's life" was as ridiculous as Theo did, and she didn't even try to hide her sarcasm.

Theo couldn't help the grin that formed on his face. He loved her feistiness. They'd never spent much time with one another at the events that brought their families together, but Theo had always noticed Alexandra. More than noticed her. When she was a young girl, she was so cute and adamant that her brothers and sister acknowledge her, no one could leave a room she was in without observing her. And then she grew into a beautiful young woman and practically stopped traffic at any function.

But as much as her physical beauty drew Theo in, it was the quiet things she did that made him want to get to know her better. The subtle side hug she gave Elliot when they were twelve when the older brothers wouldn't let him in the rugby game. Or the way she listened to the people speaking to her no matter how unimportant they seemed to the world, she always gave her full attention instead of looking around for a better conversational partner. Those and a slew of other moments were what had him throwing his reputation and heart on the line by asking her parents to be able to court her, even though to her they might have seemed virtually strangers.

"But really I was lucky to receive this assignment." The second sentence was said much more quietly and without any of the former attitude. And there was her sweetness. The woman was a perfect mix of fire and sugar that made Theo crave some crème brûlée. Actually, it just made him crave Alexandra.

But trying to get to know Alexandra had worked so well for him the first time around. He needed to get back to the task at hand. "My schedule is pretty straight forward. I'll have my assistant print you off a copy and you'll get it at least twelve hours before the first item on the calendar."

Alexandra nodded.

"There will be events that I will attend by myself, some with my parents, and maybe a few with my...." His voice trailed off. He and Elise weren't official, by any means, but Alexandra didn't need to know that. In fact, he would love to see how she felt if he and Elise were together, so he finished, "girlfriend."

Theo watched Alexandra's reaction carefully as he said the last word. And he was intrigued to see a range of emotions play out over her face. Her eyes went narrow for a split second before a subtle eye roll was covered with the half smile that had been on her face since he'd started speaking.

He was pleasantly surprised to see that Alexandra couldn't hide her emotions to save her life, so at least he'd be able to amuse himself with her reactions while he was being tortured by her presence. Okay, "tortured" was too strong a word; "thoroughly put out" would be a better term. There was nothing worse than having the only woman ever to turn him down be thrown in his path over and over. But he was a prince, for goodness' sake. He could handle it.

"That sounds perfect," Alexandra said in a monotone voice.

"Do you have any questions?" Theo asked.

Alexandra shook her head, and Theo stood to walk her to the door. She may have run from the thought of courting him, but he would still be the gentleman he was raised to be.

"You must be proud of that cover," Alexandra said, her eyebrows raising toward the life-sized copy of the photo that had graced the cover of *Celebrity Magazine* when he'd been named sexiest man of the year.

He felt heat rise to his face and he covered the dryness in his throat that her question caused with a cough. Dang, he really needed to take that thing down.

"Do you have any brothers?" Theo asked.

Alexandra's eyes went wide for not even a second before she schooled her face again.

"A couple," she answered.

"Then you know what kind of practical jokers they can be."

"They were probably jealous you got the cover to yourself," Alexandra said, and she bit her lip as soon as she finished, as if she regretted what she'd said.

Theo chose to ignore the fact that she wished her words hadn't been heard and said, "You do understand brothers."

Alexandra laughed, a deep rumbling that came from her core and filled the room with immediate joy. He'd forgotten the sound of her low-pitched, rich laughter. Never the giggle of other girls, Alexandra didn't laugh for the sake of others, so you knew you'd won something when you caused it.

He realized these kinds of moments were the last thing they needed to experience together and had to get her out of his office. Now.

"Theo," his office door shot open and revealed his mother. "And Alex, correct?"

He'd never been so grateful to have his mother barge into a private moment.

Alexandra nodded as she pushed her glasses up on her face and folded her arms.

"I'm glad I caught you here. I know that most of your colleagues will be meeting together for dinner tonight, but since we'll be spending so much time together, we hoped you, Emmalee, and Cory would join us in the formal family dining room. Your colleagues will use the casual family dining room."

"Dinner?" Alexandra asked. Her eyes flitted from Theo to Queen Marla. Her face told him joining his family for dinner was the last thing she wanted to do, but the queen seemed oblivious.

"We'll be starting in," the queen looked at her watch, "exactly six hours. Thank you for joining us."

She rushed away, probably not even realizing Alexandra hadn't actually answered, and left Alexandra with no one to look at except for Theo. She was biting her lip again, and instead of enjoying her discomfort, Theo couldn't help feeling compassion.

"Just think of it as an early start to your assignment," Theo said, since he knew the interns were told their first full day of work would be the next day.

"Do you think-" Alex started.

Theo shook his head before she could finish. "She'll hunt you down."

Alexandra's face lit up with a genuine smile, pushing her adorable full cheeks up.

"I guess I'll be seeing you in a few hours," Alexandra said as she left Theo's office.

THEO WALKED toward the room Elise was staying in for her visit. It was on the fifth floor with the rest of the family bedrooms, but all the way down the hall from Theo's in the guest bedroom wing.

He thought about Elise and her demure, but cheery ways. She was never without her smile and knew just how to compliment Theo. She was calm and settled. Unlike the vivacity that threatened to burst out of Alex any time she spoke or even made a facial expression. He couldn't imagine Alex being very free with her compliments, but he knew when she gave one it was completely sincere.

He remembered the two he received over the years. One was when she was eight and she said he looked very grown up in his tuxedo. In an eight-year-old's language, "grown up" was basically a synonym for handsome, hot, good looking, or all of the above. The other was when she was eighteen. She hadn't been very friendly to any of his brothers that trip, not even Elliot, but seemed to really have it out for Theo. If she thought that would deter him from falling for her, she'd been so wrong. It had the opposite effect. He'd already thought she was beautiful, but watching her spar with his brothers and going toe-to-toe with him had been a sight to behold. And then when she thought no one was watching, she did things like help one of the maids carry a load that was too much for one person or play a game with one of her nieces. It was during one of those games that she had spoken the other compliment to the little girl. Her niece had started crying when her little boy cousin threw the game board they'd been using up in the air. She had said all princes were awful and then turned to her aunt and asked her to agree with her. Alex had looked around the crowded sitting room and noticed everyone engrossed in their own conversations. Theo was on the couch behind her pretending to listen to the girl he'd been dating at the time go on about something or other. "Not all princes," Alex had said. "Name one," her niece had challenged. "Prince Theo," Alex had responded, and Theo's heart had soared.

Theo shook his head, realizing he'd been stuck in his memories for so long that he'd walked right past Elise's room. Feeling foolish for more than one reason, he backtracked and knocked on her door.

"Theo," Elise said happily as she clasped her hand on his arm and smiled up at him.

"Ready for dinner?" he asked.

She nodded enthusiastically, probably a bit too enthusiastically considering it was a meal they ate every day, but Theo returned her smile.

"The interns will be joining us tonight," Theo said, unsure of why he was telling Elise. Guests at dinner wasn't an unusual occurrence, but for some reason he felt the need to warn her.

"That should be nice," Elise said in her signature way. She made everything so easy.

Elise went on to tell him about the conversation she'd had

with her sister on the phone that afternoon and they were soon at the family gathering room. His mother liked everyone to be seated at the dining table at the same time, so no one left the gathering room until everyone invited to dinner arrived.

"So, tell me again why Theo needs to have a photographer at all times, but us lesser brothers can do with having one a few afternoons a week?" Theo's third brother, Seb, asked their mother with a straight face, the gleam in his eye giving him away. Seb never gave up the chance to elicit a laugh from the group, whether with a joke or at the expense of someone else.

The queen had dealt with Seb's humor for enough years that she knew exactly where he wanted her to go and she went in the opposite direction. "Because he's the favorite and best out of all of you. Why would I need to get as many photos of those who won't inherit the crown? Our posterity won't care about any of you."

The room erupted in laughter, Seb's louder than the rest, when the door to the gathering room opened to let in Alex, Cory, and Emmalee.

"Looks like we missed a joke," Emmalee said, moving into an open spot between Tristan and Elliot. Theo could have judged her type from a mile away and wasn't surprised to see that since she saw he was taken, she moved on to the other princes in the home.

"Don't worry. It was just Seb being made the butt of a joke. Being here for a whole dinner, there will be plenty more opportunities to witness that, gorgeous," Tristan said to Emmalee, causing the girl to lose her breath. She looked on the verge of fainting.

All of the brothers appreciated the lure they had over the opposite sex, but none of them used it as much as Tristan. Poor Emmalee had no idea how many times Tristan had used that same term of endearment on all kinds of women. Probably at least ten that same day.

Theo looked to Elise to share the joke with her, but she seemed to be unaware and was typing something into her phone. Still wanting someone to enjoy the moment with, he looked toward Elliot but was stopped when he saw Alex. The slight flare of her nostrils told him she was doing everything in her power not to laugh. Theo watched her until Alex looked in his direction and mouthed, "Gorgeous."

Alex let out a loud guffaw that she covered with a hacking cough that sounded like she might spit out an organ.

"Are you alright, dear?" Queen Marla asked, and Alex nodded as soon as she finished coughing. "Good. Well, since we're all here. Let's move to the dining room," she continued.

Although the custom was a bit out of date, the king always escorted his wife to dinner. It was cheesy and romantic and all of the princes knew they would continue the custom with their own wives one day.

"May I escort the lady," Seb said in a high-pitched voice as he offered his arm to Alex, causing her to finally let out the laughter she'd been keeping pent up. She went on a bit too much for the one line Seb had thrown out but couldn't seem to help herself.

She shook her head once as she passed Theo as if telling him payback would be coming.

Tristan offered his arm to Emmalee and the girl was halfway to falling in love. Tristan needed to watch his step if he didn't want a grade-A clinger in his near future.

Cory followed the couple with Elliot a few steps behind.

Theo held out his arm to Elise and they followed the group into the dining room.

Everyone was seated by the time Theo and Elise entered the room, and he saw that his mother had reserved the seat across from him for Elise. He led Elise to her spot between Cory and Seb before taking his seat in the middle of his mother and Alex.

As the first course was served, Theo listened to the conversations surrounding him. Elise was asking Seb questions about his military life while his mother and father spoke about their days and what was on the schedule for the upcoming week or so. But it was the conversation beside him that held his attention.

"What part of the United States are you from?" Tristan asked Alex.

"Alabama," Alex said, almost too quietly for Theo to hear.

"I'm a big fan of the American south," Tristan said.

"I'm from Georgia," Emmalee said, her accent sounding a bit thicker than it had a few moments earlier.

Alex's nose did the flare thing it had earlier and Theo smiled at her attempt to keep her laughter at bay. She'd probably been a first-hand witness to many types of Emmalees over the years with her own brothers.

She turned her attention to Emmalee, but she was the only one looking in the girl's direction. Tristan and Elliot both had their eyes firmly on Alex.

"Pardon, but I didn't hear where you said you were from," Elliot said to Alex.

"Alabama," Tristan answered for Alex. Elliot glared at Tristan and Tristan pretended he didn't see it. Theo wondered if Tristan was playing at an interest in Alex to show Emmalee he was an equal opportunity flirt or if he really had an interest in Alex. Judging by Elliot's glare, he seemed at least a bit interested, and Theo didn't like the growling of jealousy in his chest those thoughts produced. Sure, he'd had a thing for Alex, okay more than a thing, since he'd asked her parents for permission to court her, but it was long over. Why should he care if anyone else seemed to like her now? He had Elise now. Sweet, considerate Elise.

"I was asking Alex," Elliot said, but Tristan continued to ignore him.

"Did you attend college in Alabama?" Tristan asked Alex.

Alex shook her head, and Theo noticed her lips had dipped into a frown. It was obvious she wanted the attention anywhere but on her and, like the fool Alex had played him to be, he rescued her.

"What about you, Emmalee? Where did you go to school?" Theo said, and no one else had the opportunity to speak for the remainder of the meal.

<h1 style="text-align:center">Seven</h1>

Alex groaned when her alarm went off at five a.m. the next morning. She cursed the ringing, the darkness that surrounded her, Theo for starting his day at six a.m., and herself for deciding to leave her life as a princess. Even with the busy schedule she'd kept as a Torre, she never woke up at five a.m.

As she showered, she contemplated what she should wear. It was her first day on the job, technically, and she was surprised she wanted to impress not only Jacques, but the Kane family. And maybe even Theo, at least a little. She decided the day called for one of the dresses Jewel had left her. Alex also felt the first urge in over a year to put on some makeup and blow dry her hair. Taking a few hours to get ready had been a daily occurrence back in Litiana, and she kind of missed it.

But continuing to hide her identity was more important than some weird, vain urge to pretty herself up for the day.

She got out of the shower, pulled her wet hair back into a braid, and put on the black knee length dress that was quite a bit more form-fitting than anything she'd ever worn in her time in the states. Her glasses completed her look whether she liked it or not.

Her clock warned her that it was five minutes to six and she had to meet Daniel, Theo's personal assistant, on the fifth floor at six.

Alex hurried to leave her room, throwing both of her camera bags over her shoulder and grabbing a pastry from the breakfast cart that had arrived a few minutes before, then ran down the hall toward the elevator. She didn't run into Emmalee or Cory on the way, so she wondered if they'd gotten to sleep in or were already hard at work.

As she waited for the elevator to open, she realized she wasn't dreading the day. It seemed like none of the family had or would ever figure out her true identity. On top of that, the idea of spending the entire day with Theo didn't cause the ratcheting anxiety it had the day before. Dinner had proven he had a sense of humor, after causing her to practically suffocate from laughter with the "gorgeous" comment. And then he'd proven himself to be a true friend when he'd drawn the attention of his family away from her, as if he knew how uncomfortable their scrutiny made her.

She walked into the elevator and felt sure of her ability to complete her task. Heck, she wouldn't complete it, she would knock it out of the park *and* knock Jacques's socks off with the quality of her candids. She would be the last person standing.

"Oh good, you're here," Daniel said as soon as Alex stepped off the elevator. He thrust a stack of papers at her as he led her down the hall. "This is Prince Theo's tentative schedule for the next week."

Alex raised her eyebrows. The weight of the papers was substantial. She had assumed this was his schedule for the entire month. She had to respect a guy that worked for his country, even if he was a pretty boy prince.

She grinned at the term she just coined, even as she knew she wasn't being fair. She'd known for years he was much more than the pretty boy facade that was painted for him.

"You'll be having long days," Daniel went on as he stopped in front of a door. "I would apologize, but we all have to do it."

Alex nodded. The long days a royal had to keep up with were maybe the first thing since her time starting Jacques's course that life as a princess had prepared her to do. Sitting in a bog to catch the perfect shot of a duck heading toward the sky, sleeping on the ancient beds in the housing they stayed at during the course, and eating food that tasted like it had been sitting in a warming tray for three days were all things she had to get used to, but a long day was like slipping back into a comfortable routine.

"I'll be around if you have any questions, but basically stay out of the way and get good pictures," Daniel said.

Alex nodded again. That sounded like the perfect job for her.

Daniel opened the door in front of them and the bright light of the room they stepped into assaulted Alex's eyes after the dim lighting in the hall they'd just left.

Alex realized the brightness of the lights was amplified because the room had mirrors on every wall. Treadmills, elliptical machines, stationary bikes, and stair climbers sat to her left and weight benches, weight machines, and a row of dumbbells sat in front of a mirror on her right.

Why was she in a gym?

She continued to scan the room, just as a shirtless figure of perfection sat up on one of the weight benches. Realizing she was in a gym should have prepared Alex for the sight she beheld, but honestly, nothing could have prepared her for a bare-chested Theo. Every line of his body defined a muscle, each one more appealing than the last. Perfection wasn't enough of a word to describe what she was seeing, but it would have to do.

She swallowed when she realized how long she'd been staring and tore her eyes away and started to open her camera bag. She was going to have to shoot him like this? Heaven help her.

It was only after having a full minute to get over what she'd seen that Alex began to feel embarrassed. Had Theo noticed her staring? She'd been so focused on his arms, chest, torso, abs ... she was losing it again. She should have looked at his face.

"Mom insisted you follow me around all day. I'm sorry to subject you to my morning workout," Theo said, causing Alex to look up. "I'm sure these pictures won't ever go public, but she's got it in her head that we need to record every moment of this month. For posterity."

His face was devoid of any mirth, so Alex had to hope he hadn't noticed her staring. Subject her? Had he looked at himself in the mirror?

Of course he had, they were surrounded by them.

The door opened and in walked a shirtless Tristan and Seb. Man, oh man, it was like she'd entered a museum of the ultimate male specimen. And she was supposed to work in this environment.

Suck it up and be a professional, Alex.

Even as she ogled the men, she was grateful Elliot wasn't among the brothers. She'd seen him stare at her one too many times the night before at dinner. She hoped he was just wondering why she needed such thick lenses on her glasses and not beginning to feel that she looked familiar to him.

"What are you guys doing up?" Theo asked, his eyes narrowing at his brothers.

"We heard Alex would be documenting this moment for posterity and decided we should show up with the better-looking part of the Kane family tree," Seb teased.

Theo rolled his eyes, and Alex found herself agreeing with him. Tristan and Seb's physiques were nothing to laugh at. In fact, Alex might have stared all day if given the chance, but Theo somehow blew them out of the water.

Alex looked at Theo from the side of her eyes just to make sure she hadn't exaggerated his wowness in her mind. The peek she allowed herself screamed that she hadn't. Holy moly, looking at him was even better the second time around.

Find your camera and start shooting, Alex.

As she fumbled through her bag to find the right lens, Alex wondered how many times she'd have to command herself to get back to work that morning.

She tried to be inconspicuous as she walked around the room and snapped shots that were definitely not up to her normal standard. But instead of using her brain to figure out which angles were best and where the bright lights wouldn't affect the outcome of her photo, she was self-conscious of her way too fancy dress and had to work hard to not appear distracted by the men in the room when she was pretty much only thinking about them.

Arg!

"Couldn't drag Elliot out of bed?" Theo asked as his brothers began to work out. Tristan moved to the row of dumbbells and began to do curls in front of the mirror while Seb shoved Theo from the weight bench and forced him to spot while he bench pressed.

"We didn't even try," Tristan replied.

Alex tried not to grin as she remembered when the princes had come to visit her family in Litiana for Mando's wedding. They'd teased Elliot mercilessly, calling him sleeping beauty, since he'd slept through one of the many luncheons before the big day.

Theo turned in her direction and Alex was grateful for the enormous camera in front of her face. Had he sensed that she found humor in the situation? He definitely had the night before. He knew mouthing the word gorgeous would get Alex to laugh. But how did he know that? She would have wondered if he had somehow figured out who she really was, but even if

Theo knew she was Alexandra Torre, he would have no idea what would make the princess laugh. They'd shared a total of less than a hundred sentences in their lifetime. Enough to be casual acquaintances, but nowhere near what one would need to know what made the other tick. Even Elliot, the brother she'd spent the most time with, didn't know her like that.

Come to think of it, did anyone know her like that? Before she was betrayed, she would have assumed Pedro, the guy she dated for three years, would have fallen into that category at some point in her life, along with Elise. But as she thought back on both relationships, even if they had lasted a while, they were mostly made of fluff. Her mother probably made that list and her brother Mando. Maybe Jane.

Alex stopped her list-making as she became more depressed by the moment. She had friends, didn't she? Growing up she had been ridiculously shy and her sister Lizzie had been the outgoing princess. Everyone loved Lizzie and they allowed Alex to tag along because the two were a package deal. But then the car accident that tore Lizzie from her life happened, and Alex was left alone.

She had mourned until Elise tried to fill the hole that Lizzie had left. Before they became friends, Alex had decided she wanted a turn at being the outgoing one. But instead of raking in the friends like Lizzie had, people seemed to be put off by Alex's blunt way of speaking and dry humor. So, Elise and Pedro were the only people to get close to Alex, until they both walked away.

And now who did she have?

"Are you getting my good side, Alex?" Seb's question pulled her from her thoughts.

"Seb's good side is me," Tristan said as he came to pose in front of where Alex stood.

Theo rolled his eyes, but the upturned quirk of his lips gave away that he was amused with his brothers' antics. Not for the first time, Alex wondered what life would have been like had Lizzie lived. Alex had plenty of brothers, but a sibling of the same sex was different. She saw the way her brothers had inside jokes that were only among the boys, and in the few hours she'd observed the Kanes, it was the same way. Alex knew she should be grateful because she had some of the best sisters-in-law in the world, but moving away had changed her relationship with them.

Okay, enough of the pity party.

Tristan flexed, first standing straight with both arms at either side Then he turned sideways and leaned over, one arm flexed in front of his body, another in back, in the classic body-builder pose.

Alex smiled as she snapped away. If this was for posterity, they would all enjoy the laugh.

"Now that amateur hour is over," Seb said as he pushed Tristan aside. What was it with boys and competition? She would say the behavior in front of her was juvenile if she hadn't witnessed the same type of behavior with her own brothers who were all grown men in their thirties and forties.

Seb turned his back to Alex and clasped his hands together allowing every muscle in his arms and back to ripple.

Alex took a few shots but stopped when she heard Theo say, "Real men don't need to pose."

Tristan threw the towel he'd been using to wipe his face at Theo's head, but the latter ducked in time.

Seeing the sweaty towel reminded Alex that the room should reek, but the air in the room was surprisingly fresh. She looked around to see how that could be but couldn't find an answer.

"Did you need something?" Theo asked as he made his way from the weight bench to the dumbbells. "Sorry if you're getting bored. I'm almost done. You can wait outside if you want."

Alex saw that his cheeks were still a bit red, almost like they were sun kissed, and she'd assumed that it was because of exertion from working out. But he hadn't done anything too exhausting in the past few minutes and the red was still there. Was the mighty pretty boy prince embarrassed to get his picture taken with his shirt off?

"Did you want me to leave? I was kind of enjoying the show," Alex asked, hoping the question would redden his cheeks a bit more.

Sure enough, the red brightened, and Alex smiled. Embarrassment made the pretty boy prince seem human which was endearing.

"You should have posed, Theo," Seb said. "Too bad you aren't part of the show that the beautiful photographer enjoyed."

Alex had been so caught up in her chat with Theo that she'd almost forgotten the other princes were even in the room, much less about their posing. She hadn't meant *that* show but didn't know how she could clarify herself without being too honest. Teasing Theo about his physique was one thing, but allowing him to think she had a crush on him, not a chance.

Wait, Theo had a girlfriend. Granted it was the evil one, Elise, but Alex didn't steal boyfriends or flirt with boyfriends. What was she doing? Maybe whatever good scent was being pumped into the gym was accompanied by a drug that was causing Alex to lose all rational sense. Prince Theo was practically her boss and an obstacle on the course to her dream job. There would be no flirting with the boss nor crushes.

Instead of responding to Seb, Alex went back to snapping photos, her job, and was grateful the camera worked as a fantastic barrier between herself and her all-too-good-looking boss.

$$\mathcal{E}ight$$

As Theo showered, he realized it might be the one activity all day he would be doing without an audience. No, there would be one more. But he'd had to fight long and hard to get that time away from the camera.

Thankfully even his mother agreed that showering was part of their lives that didn't need to be captured for posterity. He quickly dressed and then made his way to his office. Poor Alex would be in for a boring morning, since paperwork would take up most of the early hours of the day.

When had he started to care about what happened to Alex? And when had he started calling her Alex?

Theo knew she was no longer the enemy he'd perceived her to be, even though it still bugged him that he didn't know why her answer to a courtship between them had been no. He hadn't been asking for forever, yet. Granted, courtship was a bit intense, but it was the way the Litians did things. Theo had heard first-hand accounts of Alex's brother Mando and his wife Lala's courtship and practically arranged marriage. What Theo had asked was low-key compared to them.

And why was Alex in hiding now? Had she been running from him? That was a bit presumptuous of him, but it was a valid question. Or maybe it wasn't about running away and she was running to something?

It had to be the latter since she hadn't run again when they bumped into each other. On top of that, she'd come across the Atlantic to live in his family home for a month. Now, they were about to spend day in and day out together, and she didn't seem completely repulsed. But it would be nice to hear the words "you didn't make me run away from home" from her mouth.

Dang, he was acting like a needy wimp.

All of that was in the past, they had a good working relationship now, and he was going to move on. Like a man.

A soft knock sounded on his door that he knew was Alex. Daniel's knock had everyone in the vicinity wondering if the walls were coming down, it was so loud, and no one else came to his office.

"Come in," Theo said, and Alex entered.

She looked around the room, grinning when she caught sight of the poster, and then walked to a corner and leaned back against the bookshelf. "Just pretend I'm not here," she said.

Fat chance. Theo really wished he could tell her she could have free time to photograph the grounds or anything other than him sitting at his desk. But his mother would be livid; she'd been adamant about Theo's entire life as the crown prince being recorded. Something about it being the best type of history. Theo should be grateful he didn't have a full camera crew following his every move.

His mother loved to think about coming generations and what they would want to know about their past relatives. It was a bit morbid, if you asked him. But this anniversary was a big one, the biggest yet, according to his mother, and Theo wasn't about to do anything to rock the boat, much less upset her, so close to her day. If he'd learned one thing about women over the years, it was to let them win the battles that mattered most to them.

The morning went by quickly for Theo, he had to wonder if Alex had been bored to tears. But he didn't see any streaming down her lovely face.

He needed to get a grip and stop thinking about how attractive the woman was. She was a woman hired to follow him around. That was it. Elise was lovely as well. He would focus on Elise's lovely face.

"Was it awful?" Theo asked as he stood, and Alex did the same. Theo had offered Alex a chair as soon as she came into his office, but she'd said she preferred to work standing. About an hour in, and at least a hundred snaps of her camera later, she'd taken him up on his offer.

"I think I got some really good shots of the wood grain in your desk," Alex said.

Theo laughed. "Maybe I can talk my mother into lessening your hours."

"No!" Alex said quickly. "This is a privilege. I'm sorry if my teasing made it seem like I wasn't pleased with my job."

"Not at all. I just assumed. You didn't say anything to make me think you weren't a professional."

Alex took in a deep breath and nodded once.

"Well, I better get going," Theo said as Alex began to follow.

"You can join the family at lunch. I'm sure there will be lots of good photo opportunities," Theo said. He was sure that the schedule Daniel had given Alex had blocked off this time. This was the one thing he'd been adamant with his mom about. No photos between eleven and one every Monday, Wednesday, and Friday.

"But...." Alex began.

"You're off duty," Theo said with a smile. "See you at one."

He hurried out of his office and down the hall without waiting for a response.

THE NEXT MORNING began the same way as the one before. His brothers awoke in time to interrupt his gym time and flirt with Alex. Poor Alex had to try to come up with new shots to take of the same activity and Theo tried not to be too embarrassed about all the pictures being taken of him with his shirt off.

It had been bad enough for the cover of *Celebrity Magazine*, but knowing Alex was the one capturing his likeness? He wasn't like his brothers who felt that shirts were only created for men with large bellies. Theo loved the attention of the fairer sex just like the other Valdorian princes, but his manner of getting it was a bit subtler than the others. His brothers called him shy, but Theo preferred to think of himself as an introvert. He didn't need the attention of every woman in the room, just the attention of the one special woman by his side.

"So, Theo," Seb started, and Theo knew nothing good could come out of his brother's mouth when he began with that cheeky grin. Seb was spotting Theo as he bench pressed, and Theo pretended he was concentrating too hard on his set to answer. "How are things with the new girl?"

Theo thought he saw Alex drop her camera an inch before hoisting it back up as if nothing had happened. That small movement, along with the way Alex had reacted during that first tea when she saw Elise, had Theo wondering what had gone on between the two of them? When Theo first saw them interact, he assumed Alex had been the cause of whatever the issue was, but now that he knew Alex a bit better and he was beyond being a bitter, moody teen about their past, he wasn't so sure. He still didn't know Alex very well, but then again, he and Elise hadn't been dating for very long. Granted, she seemed sweet and moldable, and maybe a bit boring?

"Great," Theo finally said, grunting as he pushed the barbell up and back onto its rack.

"Hm, that didn't sound very convincing. Did it, Alex?" Seb asked.

Alex shook her head as she silently moved backward, the international sign for 'I'm not getting involved'.

Seb laughed. "Did it, Tristan?"

"No. It really didn't." Tristan gave the answer Seb was waiting for.

"So if it's not going great, there are other options. Good, for one. Bad, for another. Are you going to tell us the truth this time, big brother?" Seb asked.

Theo pushed off of the bench and moved to dumbbells. He didn't have time for his brother's inane questions. He had a line-up of appearances that began in two hours and he still had to shower, get photographed at breakfast, and drive to the first location of the day.

"Looks like he isn't," Tristan said with a smile.

"So, we'll have to guess what's going on." Seb rubbed his hands together as his grin widened. "The new girl is cute. I'll have to give her that. Not as beautiful as our photographer girl, but okay nonetheless," Seb said.

Theo heard Alex grunt before she moved as far as she could from Seb while still remaining in the gym.

"I've had one conversation with her, so I can only judge her based on that, but she seems a little light in the banter department. That means I'd have to put one check in the negative column. So far, I'd say we are well on our way to average. The death of every relationship," Seb continued.

Theo narrowed his eyes at his brother, not because he was wrong, but because he was right. He hated it when that happened. Now he would start to analyze every move Elise made and find her lacking. He should probably break up with her now and get it over with. Stupid Seb.

"But what if Elise is as good as it gets for our Theo?" Tristan asked, his grin matching Seb's.

Theo fought the urge to smack the grins off of both their faces, but the worst thing he could do was react. So, he kept a straight face and continued to curl one arm, then the other.

"You have a point there, brother. Theo doesn't have the greatest track record and seems to attract the beautiful but, in all other aspects, average type," Seb agreed.

Theo dropped the weights with a thud and moved to the leg machine. One more set and he was out of there.

"He did choose well once," Tristan said with a gleam in his eye.

Theo was going to kill them and his mother would in turn kill him. But then again, did any mother really need four sons? She could be happy with two.

Theo fought to keep from having any type of emotion show on his face or even in his demeanor. He knew what was coming would be embarrassing, but at least his brothers couldn't reveal anything Alex didn't already know. She knew he had tried to court her. It would just be an awkward moment and then they could move on.

"Alexandra Torre," Seb picked up where Tristan left off.

Theo heard a thud and looked up in the mirror to see Alex sitting on one of the treadmills.

"You okay, photography girl?" Seb asked.

Alex nodded, but kept the camera in front of her face the entire time.

"Now she was a spitfire. Funny, interesting, all things Theo's girlfriends aren't," Seb said.

Theo fought the urge to roll his eyes.

"Proposed and got shot down," Tristan said, shaking his head and laughing.

"But what did he expect? He asked her *parents* to court her. Who does that?" Seb said, joining in the laughter.

"I was trying to be respectful of their customs," Theo muttered under his breath, since he'd used the same line on his brothers all of the other many times they'd hassled him.

"And it still goes back to the average type being the only type to be attracted to him. Alexandra was out of his league by a long shot," Tristan said.

He had to agree with him on that one.

"I wonder what the beautiful princess is up to these days," Seb said.

Theo watched in the mirror as Alex ran into a stationary bike but continued moving like she hadn't.

"Not getting engaged to our brother," Tristan teased.

"You should find her, Theo. Ask again. Anything is better than another day dating the queen of the mundane," Seb said.

"Even if she did agree to date him, which I'm pretty sure the hot spot where the devil resides would have to freeze over before that happened, Mom would never let it happen," Tristan added helpfully.

Theo finished his set and started for the door. It was time for this session of "embarrass Theo" to be finished.

"I forgot! She hates the girl," Seb said, starting to laugh again.

Alex followed Theo toward the door with wide eyes. He felt bad that she'd heard the last part. If he had known the conversation would veer in that direction, he'd have gotten out of there sooner.

When Theo realized he was more worried about Alex's feelings than his own, and hadn't even considered Elise, he also realized his earlier thought was spot on. He should break up with Elise.

He looked at Alex's face and wished there was something he could do to make her feel better. But he was pretty sure there wasn't, not without revealing he knew who she was. And at some point, he'd come to the agreement with himself that he would only acknowledge Alex's true identity when and if she told him. He assumed it was more than likely to never happen.

"I'm sorry," he said, and paused, hoping she felt some comfort in those words. Then continued, "I need to do something of a personal nature for the next few minutes. I know you were supposed to shoot me at breakfast this morning, but can I get a raincheck? I can meet you at the car in an hour and a half?"

Alex nodded, and Theo imagined she was replaying his brothers' conversation in her head.

Theo waited for Alex to get to the elevator before walking down the hall to the room Elise was staying in.

As he walked, he wondered if he was being too hasty. Had he let his brothers get in his head and talk him into something that he didn't want to do? Sure, Elise wasn't Alex, but no woman was. And who was to say Alex was the right one for him, anyway?

But the reason he was listening to his brothers was because they had valid points.

On the other hand, his brothers were also known for exaggerating. There were lots of good things about Elise they hadn't brought up.

But then again, she wasn't exactly a sparkling conversationalist, and wasn't that important to Theo? It was better to break up with her now, while no one was attached.

As he argued with himself, he reached her door while the thoughts to break up with Elise were winning. He knocked on the door, sweat that had nothing to do with his workout beginning to bead up on his face. This was the only downside to dating lots of good looking women.

"Oh, Theo," Elise said happily as she opened the door. "This is a pleasant surprise. I thought I was supposed to meet you at the car in," she looked down at her dainty wrist that held a small gold watch, "an hour and thirty-seven minutes."

Theo brought a hand up to rub the back of his neck. "Um," he said as he looked at the door, the doorway, in the room behind Elise, basically anywhere other than at the girl herself.

"Oh," he heard Elise say quietly, and he looked down to see her shift her weight from one foot to the other.

"You're a nice girl," Theo started.

"Let's not do this," Elise said, causing Theo to look right at her. "It's awkward for you and awkward for me. I get it."

Theo dropped his hand from his neck and tilted his head as he narrowed his eyes. It couldn't be that easy, could it? He'd never gone through a break up without tears or screaming or both.

"We weren't even technically official, right?" Elise said with a smile.

Maybe she wasn't as stuck in her ways as Theo originally thought, and when she smiled, it really brightened her face. And another point in her favor, this was the best conversation he'd ever had during a break-up. Maybe he hadn't given her a chance to show her conversation skills? He hadn't given her a chance to show much of anything.

"You're making this really easy." Theo said the words, and as he said them, he wondered if they would set her off. Something had to. She was too eerily calm.

"Why make it difficult? If we aren't compatible, we aren't compatible."

"I didn't say we weren't compatible," Theo said, feeling himself waver even more. Sure, Elise was no Alexandra Torre, but maybe Theo had built Alexandra up in his mind. Actually, he knew he had. No woman could be as perfect as the Alexandra in his mind. He'd only had a few interactions with her, and then she'd denied him. It could possibly be a case of wanting what he couldn't get. Girls usually flocked to him, and she'd run away. And even if he stopped dating Elise, that didn't mean he would pursue Alex. She'd made her choice and didn't seem to be regretting it.

Besides, his brothers were wrong. Elise wasn't like all of the other girls he'd dated. She was proving that now, and Theo needed to be a man about this, not the boy from his past relationships. It was time for him to date a girl more seriously than he had in the past, not dump the one who seemed different from all the rest.

"What did you say?" Elise asked. They both knew he'd said nothing, but his actions had said a whole lot.

"I like you," Theo said. Going back on what he'd already said would be tough. How would he make it up to her?

Elise bit her lip and nodded.

She was agreeing. That was good. But she still wasn't happy with him.

"You were right. We haven't made this official and I'd like to change that," Theo said.

Elise's smile spread from ear to ear.

"I want to ask if you'd join us for some of the photos we'll be in today. Stand by my side. As my...." Theo paused. Once he said that word, there was no going back. "Girlfriend."

Elise nodded. "I'd love to."

Theo nodded in return, and as he walked away, his throat went dry as he wondered what the heck had happened. He'd always been so decisive in the past. He always knew what he wanted. But somehow in the past few days, he'd become a pile of putty in the hands of every woman in his life, and this time his pendulum of indecisiveness had swung so wide that he was doing the exact opposite of what he'd set out to do. The worst part was, he had no idea how to go back to the man he was.

How had he gone from going to break up with Elise to making their relationship so official that they were going to grace the cover of every international magazine?

Nine

"You can't come with me," Alex said as Jane followed her into her bedroom.

"Of course, I can. It's my job," Jane said.

Alex walked into her closet and scanned the clothes, noticing that Jewel must have added more clothing to her wardrobe. She threw off the slacks and top she wore in favor of a dark blue maxi dress. It would be dark enough to blend into the background but nice enough for the ceremony she'd be attending.

"Jane," Alex said as she walked back into the bedroom, "you can't come to every event outside of the castle with me. That would surely raise suspicions."

"I wouldn't be much of a bodyguard if I didn't," Jane countered.

"The royal family will have plenty of their own guards."

"Who aren't going to be looking out for you."

"Jane," Alex said, blowing out a puff of air.

"Alex," Jane mimicked.

"The family hardly notices me now, but if you come with me, I'll have to make special arrangements everywhere I go.

They're sure to start wondering why," Alex said. "You'll blow the cover we worked so long to build."

Mando had promised Alex when she applied that no one would ever know her true identity. After Alex entered the program on her own merit, Jane was let into the program as a special favor to the Litian royal family. Everyone, including Jacques, was under the impression that Jane was the little sister of one of Mando's best friends whose dream was to be a world class photographer. Mando pulled some strings with Jacques as a favor to his "friend" and then had a hacker arrange the room assignments so that Jane and Alex would stay together. Mando had been assured that Jane would be a part of the program, even the internship portion, but would not receive the job at the end. Alex was grateful for that since, if Jane was assured the job, Alex would have no shot at it. Mando asked Alex how she'd be guarded if she landed the job, but Alex figured they could cross that bridge later. If and when she were hired as a result of her own skill, she wouldn't care if the whole world knew her identity. She just had to make it to that point with no one knowing. She couldn't have this accomplishment tainted by the possibility that anyone knew she was a Torre. Her last name would give her any and everything if she let it. But it also made her feel like nothing was her own.

"I'd rather have *you* safe than the cover safe," Jane said.

Alex rolled her eyes. "What kind of danger could possibly be lurking at a ribbon cutting ceremony for a new cancer research center?"

"An upset employee? A gunman who feels the charity money should have been used in another way? Anyone who's ever been disgruntled with the Valdorian royal family? Need I go on?"

Alex lowered her head as she put a hand to her forehead. "Seriously? You are in the wrong line of work. With an imagination like that, you should be writing movies."

Jane grunted in disagreement.

"So, you're going to follow me around like a shadow now? You've always given me so much space," Alex said, knowing her voice had gone in a bit too high as she pled. But she was feeling as desperate as the squeak in her voice sounded.

"The other students in the course were vetted and we've only been in the castle up until this point, one of the most secure buildings on the planet." Jane explained her past actions.

Alex sighed loudly. "I still don't get why Chandler was able to leave Litiana guardless. You know it's just because I'm a girl," Alex said.

"Don't try to use girl power on me," Jane said with a disappointed head tilt.

Alex huffed. It had been worth a try.

Jane narrowed her eyes as she watched Alex sulk. "Why is this so important to you?"

Alex shook her head. "You wouldn't understand."

"Try me."

Alex sighed, not sure why she was going to give in because she was sure she already knew the outcome. "I've been handed everything in my life. People tell me I'm beautiful, but I've had teams of staff around me to dress me, do my hair, teach me makeup skills. I've been told I'm smart, but I had the best tutors money could buy. I was about nine and I'd been given my semester grades and they were all A's. I was thrilled. I was in the process of hurrying to show them to my mom when Bernard, a guy my brother Chandler's age, started laughing. That stopped me in my tracks, and I turned around with the sassiest stance I could muster and glared at him. "You don't actually think you've earned those grades, do you?" he'd asked. "Your parents pay these people. Of course they're going to tell you you're amazing." I was about to continue running to my mom, ignoring Bernard because he'd always been a jerk, when Lizzie jumped in. She went on and on about how I really was smart and who did Bernard think he was. But as she defended me, I suddenly realized what Bernard said was the truth. Lizzie was trying to guard my feelings. It was then that I concluded that any accolade I received wouldn't come because I was Alexandra, it would come because I was a Torre." Alex made eye contact with Jane. "I know, poor pampered princess, right?"

Jane didn't say anything, so Alex decided to go on. Might as well.

"But photography. No one thought of it as anything other than a hobby, so I wasn't gifted the finest tutors. Everything I know about photography I learned from books, YouTube, and any other resources a normal, everyday person could get their hands on. People would smile at my pictures and say they were good, but I didn't truly believe it until I got into Jacques's course. He didn't know who I was and I got in. My pictures spoke to him, and I was finally succeeding at something no one had given me."

Alex looked up at Jane's face and saw the same blank expression. "Yeah, that's what I thought," Alex said. " I get it. My life isn't tough. You're the one who asked me to tell you."

Jane was still staring at Alex.

"So, what's the plan?" Alex asked. "Are you going to use the Litian royal seal and tell Jacques that you need to see every event outside of the castle for whatever reason Mando's best friend's little sister would need to be there?"

Jane drew in a deep breath. "Nope," she finally said.

"So, what then?" Alex asked as she walked toward the door.

"You'll go to the event on your own."

Alex stopped in her tracks. "What did you say?"

Jane shook her head as if she couldn't believe she was about to say the words, but continued, "I'm not going to go with you. Your secret will stay safe."

"Seriously?" Alex asked.

Jane nodded. "But you better swear that you'll be careful."

Alex rushed at Jane and threw her arms around her. Jane remained stiff, and Alex laughed before she said, "I'll stay with the Valdorian guard at all times. They'll become my best friends."

"And if someone tries to steal your camera?" Jane asked. She knew Alex cared for nothing more than the Canon baby that hung around her neck.

"I'll send them off with well-wishes," Alex said.

Jane nodded. "I better get to portrait class," she said before walking past Alex. "Please don't make me regret this," she added before closing the door behind her.

Alex stuffed a mini quiche from her breakfast cart into her mouth and then grabbed all of her equipment before following Jane out of her room. This was going to be a good day.

It wasn't until Alex was seated in the front seat of the town car Theo and Elise rode in that she remembered what Theo's brothers had said. They almost made it seem like Theo had been the one to ask to court Alex, not his parents. But what kind of young guy worked through those kinds of channels to get a girl to like him? If he really liked her, wouldn't he have come to her, not her parents? The whole thing was strange, and she wondered what her life would have been like if she'd given Theo a chance.

But even though she felt a tinge of jealousy as she saw Elise grab Theo's hand out of the corner of her eye, she knew it wouldn't have worked with her and Theo. Even if, and that was a big if, Theo had wanted her, photography was her top passion. Being the wife of a crown prince, heck the girlfriend of a crown prince, left no time or energy for any other kind of passion.

She'd gotten away with a lot being the seventh child, but Lala, her brother Mando's wife, had to be a future queen first and foremost. Everything else fell by the wayside.

Alex remembered that it was her job to catch every moment, and she turned to snap a few photos of the happy couple behind her. Theo was breathtakingly handsome in his gray suit. His dark hair and naturally tan complexion looked good with any color, but something about gray made his clear blue eyes look extra blue and it created a perfect picture. Strictly professionally speaking.

Elise's red dress seemed a bit much for a daytime ribbon cutting ceremony, but as she nestled in under Theo's arm, Alex had to admit they looked good together. Really good. Elise's long blond hair and fair skin were the opposite of Theo in every way, creating a stunning photo.

Alex gritted her teeth. Man, she hated that girl.

She remembered a slumber party where Elise was brushing Alex's hair and told her that she was so envious of her dark hair. She'd said something along the lines of hating her blond hair since she could never tell which boys liked her for her or because her hair was so gorgeous. Alex had laughed at the comment thinking it was such an Elise thing to say. That should have been her first sign that her "best" friend was a self-centered, backstabbing brat.

Alex shook her head. She'd spent enough of her life dwelling on memories of herself and Elise, wondering where it could have gone wrong.

"Since these are going to be our first official photos, shouldn't we have someone other than the photography student take them?" Elise asked.

Alex bit down on her tongue so hard she worried she might actually sever it in half to keep from telling Elise just where she could stick her opinions.

"Alex and the other interns are some of the top photographers in the world," Theo said, looking up from his phone at Elise for a minute before turning his attention back to whatever he was doing. He didn't seem upset, just somewhat amused that Elise was so misinformed. Alex knew how easy it was to be deceived by Elise. She'd been the one to be amused a few years ago.

But now Alex knew better. Elise wasn't misinformed, she just had to do her best to put down any female around her so that she could be a head above everyone else in the room.

Alex took in a breath and then let it out slowly. She'd need to let go of the past and any of her feelings about Elise if she wanted to get through the rest of this internship. Elise could cuddle up to Theo and marry the guy for all Alex cared. Alex just needed to remind herself that the job with Jacques was even more crucial than putting Elise in her place.

Although, seeing that girl get hers would be so fun. But not worth it if it cost Alex the chance at her dream job, she had to remind herself.

"You know, maybe today isn't the best day for us to take public pictures of our relationship," Theo said.

Alex turned slightly to see that he still had his eyes on his phone. She saw Elise's face pinch before she smoothed it out quickly. Theo missed the whole thing.

"Sure. Whatever you think is best," Elise said with a smile.

"It's just, I think I was a bit hasty in my decision. Today should be about the cancer research center. If we show up together, it would take the focus off of what's important."

"Of course." Alex heard the strain in Elise's voice that seemed to go right over Theo's head.

"I knew you'd understand," Theo said as he patted Elise's knee.

Alex turned forward before either person could notice that she had witnessed the entire exchange. Well, if that was the kind of woman Theo wanted in his life, it was a great thing Alex had run when she had. She was nothing like the Elise that sat behind her. Willing to step on her friends to get into relationships where she agreed with everything the man said. No, thank you.

Ten

Theo felt badly about leaving Elise in the backseat of the black SUV while he and Alex got out, but as he had scrolled through his emails, he'd seen how hard the cancer treatment center had worked to receive publicity today. He couldn't overshadow that. Also, his decision might have had a bit to do with the sour feeling in his gut that coming out into the limelight with Elise was exactly the opposite of what he should be doing. As he reflected on his actions in the last few days, he realized what he needed to do was find a good middle ground for everyone involved. This seemed like it was it. Keep Elise in his life, but take it slow. No rash choices for this guy.

Was he like this with every relationship he'd been in? No. He'd always been so sure of each decision he made. So, what was different now? He knew the difference had to do with the havoc a certain female was creating in him.

But what *had* stayed the same from his past was that he had never felt completely confident in any woman he dated. That's why he broke up with them. He just wished he could finally feel sure of a woman. Maybe he hadn't given any of them enough time? But with Alexandra....

You're an idiot, Theo.

Alexandra turned him down. It was the only reason she'd gotten under his skin. Theo had never dealt well with rejection.

He shook his mind free of the women both in and out of his life before applying his public smile. He knew the cameras had already started clicking and he needed to do his job.

Daniel was by his side and leading him toward the tent that had been set up by the cancer center entrance. The press waiting under the tent had been personally invited, and the center had put the tent up to make sure any roving helicopters out for a perfect photo of the royal heir wouldn't get it. There had been rumors about him and Elise, and every news rag wanted the first photo. Seeing the tent made him even more grateful he'd left Elise in the car.

"We're so grateful you could make it," a woman in a tight black skirt and matching suit coat said as she took Theo's hand.

"Marion Phillips, biggest patron of the center," Daniel whispered in Theo's ear. Daniel was the exact same height as Theo's six-foot-three, another reason he was the perfect assistant. No one knew when Daniel fed Theo information.

"Ms. Phillips. A pleasure," Theo said.

He noticed that Alex had kept to the other side of them, snapping picture after picture. No one else seemed to notice she was there, but Theo couldn't get her out of his mind.

It wasn't until Daniel moved between Theo and Marion that Theo noticed how the woman had pressed against his side. Women getting too close was a daily occurrence for Theo, and Daniel somehow managed them all. Another reason he was worth every penny Theo paid him.

Daniel swore under his breath as he held his earpiece, and several of Theo's bodyguards swarmed toward him.

Theo glanced around the room to try to discover the threat that had caused the commotion.

"It's a code green," Daniel said as he and the guards guided Theo and a wide-eyed Alex back toward the cars they'd come in. "Your SUV just took Elise back to the castle, but we have two of the decoys still here."

"I don't want to miss the ceremony for a code green," Theo said, knowing how important it was to the center that he make an appearance that morning. The news coverage would do wonders for the amount of donations that would come in, and he knew every penny would be put to good use. The center was already being hailed as one of the best in the world and had drawn in renowned doctors from many nations. Now they needed the funds to keep them there.

"Hopefully you won't miss it. We need to assess the threat and try to start with just a few minute delay," Daniel said before he shoved Theo from behind into the SUV. Theo felt a body fall onto his legs as he tried to move out of the doorway and knew from the shape and weight that it had to be Alex. He turned himself in order to help Alex into the car as the door slammed shut behind them and two of his guards jumped into the front seats. Then the car peeled out of the parking lot.

As Alex sat up straight beside him, Theo took in her demeanor. Her mouth wasn't smiling nor frowning, and she turned her head to look out the window at what they were leaving.

"I'm sorry if they manhandled you," Theo said as the car took them to the predesignated safe area his bodyguards had scouted long before they'd arrived at the event.

"Jane would have been proud," Alex muttered.

"What was that?" Theo asked.

"Nothing," Alex said, and Theo wished he could read her thoughts. Her face was blank, her posture was moderate, neither relaxed nor charged. She seemed ready for anything.

After she finished examining the view out the window, she turned her attention to her camera.

"Is it okay?" Theo asked, scooting toward her to look at the expensive piece of equipment.

Alex nodded, her appearance still giving away nothing. "What's a code green?" she asked.

"An extra person is in the vicinity. Any event at which a royal appears at is by invitation only. If the number of invitations collected and the number of people at the event don't match up...."

"It's a code green," Alex finished.

Theo nodded as he sat on the edge of his seat. He was still expecting the hysterics to happen at any moment. He'd been in quite a few code whatever situations with women by his side, and the hysterics happened every single time. He'd dated celebrities, other royals, and most every type of woman, so his pool of knowledge in the area was quite large.

Being reminded of the women he dated, Theo realized he should send a text to Elise and let her know he was alright in case she heard chatter about the incident.

I'm glad you're safe. She texted back. With another almost immediate follow-up. *I think I'm going to go home for a bit. I know you felt like it was time to go public, but as I thought about it, I think it would be best to wait until your parents' anniversary celebration is over.*

Theo let out a sigh of relief. Of course, Elise was on the same page he was. And she really did think of everything. Not only should they take it slow, he couldn't steal his parents' thunder like that. She seemed so perfect and yet...his relief at her leaving should be screaming at him to reconsider their breakup. But she'd be out of his life for a bit, long enough for him to get Alex out of his system. Then she could come back and Theo could really get to know Elise without being in Alex's shadow. Alex had to be the problem. Everything about Elise was so right, on paper.

Theo heard Alex turn on the leather seat next to him, pulling his attention back to the car. And even as he knew he shouldn't be caring about her, he couldn't help asking, "Are you alright?" He was doing what any gentleman would do. Plus, he really wanted to know the answer. Most women would be falling apart in this situation, and he needed to know Alex was like other women.

"It's nothing I'm not used to," Alex said before she sucked in a sharp breath. "I meant it's nothing I can't imagine being used to. I have a very vivid imagination."

That was the closest to a slip up Alex had ever had in front of him, so the code green was having an effect on her. She was just doing an amazing job of acting composed. So, she was both like the other women in his life and not like them. That wasn't helping him in his quest to get over her. He decided to go with small talk. No one fell in deeper like over small talk.

"Imagination can be useful in your line of work, I suppose," Theo said. He felt the car park and knew that they could be waiting for anywhere between ten minutes and a few hours. He really hoped it was closer to the first number. Being locked in a car with Alex wasn't exactly on his list of smart ideas.

Alex nodded. "Sometimes I'll think of perfect frames or scenes as I'm falling asleep at night and then try to recreate them the next day," she said quietly, but her face had changed from blank to glowing.

"You love what you do," Theo stated. There was no question about it.

"It's the only thing that's mine," Alex said, and the glow left her face as her cheeks reddened. She hadn't meant to say that either. Theo was finding he enjoyed an unguarded Alex.

"Elise seems nice," Alex said, her jaw clenched as she said the words.

Theo tried not to grin at the obvious lie she told or at her abrupt change of conversation topics. Maybe unguarded Alex would shed some light on why she wasn't a fan of Elise. Theo hated to admit it, but if he found out Alex didn't dislike his girl-friend like he thought she did, it would make him a lot more comfortable in the relationship. Why should he care what Alex thought?

"She is." Theo hoped giving as little information would get Alex to give more.

"How did you two meet?"

"You signed the nondisclosure agreement, correct?" Theo asked with a grin.

"Yes, sir," Alex said with a salute. There was her sass.

"My mother and her mother are friends."

"You met through your moms?" Alex's left eyebrow nearly met her hairline.

"Not through them, exactly. We met at a function we all attended."

Theo caught Alex bite her lip and knew she was trying not to laugh at him.

"And she wasn't dating anyone?" Alex asked after she gained control of her laughter.

That was a strange question. "I didn't think so. But we weren't dating exclusively until...." Theo stopped. Were they dating exclusively? He'd lied about it to Alex the day before, and then that morning he had basically said that they were a couple to Elise, but now that they'd both taken a step back. He found he wasn't having fun dwelling on his relationship.

"Why do you ask?" Theo tried to turn the tables on Alex, still working to get a glimpse into Alex and Elise's past.

When she didn't answer, Theo suddenly felt sick of the games he was playing. He decided to man up and straight out ask her what he wanted to know. "Do you know Elise?"

"Me, no." Alex sat up straight against the back of the car. "How would I, I mean, no. No, I don't know her."

"Okay," Theo said as he raised his hands beside his head. Her answer was defensive and she knew it.

Dang, he should have taken a slower approach. Her reaction only proved that she did know Elise, and now she'd never reveal the truth. But then again, she had been silent when he'd asked his last question. She probably wouldn't have given him any information anyway. He could always ask Elise, but that might reveal Alex's identity and... his life was messier than he wanted to admit.

Alex turned her head to look out the window. "How long can these things take?" she asked.

"In a crowd the size we left, probably an hour. They have to match people to invitations, staff to lists, etc."

Alex nodded and shifted closer to the door.

What was it with this woman? Theo didn't usually mention to anyone the type of effect he had on women, but Alex's reaction wasn't it. She couldn't wait to get out of the car. Call it his pride, but Theo needed to change that.

He slid down the seat so that his shoulder touched Alex's.

"So, Alex," he said, lowering his voice. He knew his brothers would call it cheesy, but this move had never failed him before. "What it is about photography that is so appealing?"

Theo had underestimated how small Alex could make herself as she shifted again so that her back was against the car door and not a single part of her body touched Theo.

He wanted to roll his eyes at his utter fail. He'd never had a woman move away from him, and he realized he had no moves because he'd never had to be the one to initiate anything. He was a twenty-nine-year-old bachelor with no game.

"It's cool," she said.

Okay, maybe his lack of moves hadn't had her fainting since all he'd done was bestow her with his undivided attention, but he deserved more than an "It's cool." Her lack of an answer motivated him to try one more time.

He started to put his arm up to wrap around her shoulders when Alex blurted, while staring at her camera, "When I see the world through my lens, I get to see what's there, or I can imagine how to make it better. The same picture can be mysterious, frightening, light, dark, shadowy, clear, depending on how I want to shoot it."

So, all he had to do was threaten her with physical touch. She was like a lumber jack to his ego.

"That's cool," Theo said, feeling more than a bit annoyed. He shifted so that he was back in his original seat.

Alex's eyes went from the camera and moved to Theo's face. He saw her take in a deep breath before she pointed out his window.

"Do you see that tree?" she asked.

He nodded as he looked to where she pointed. They were parked along a maple tree-lined street with homes that were built sometime in the past fifty years. Alex had pointed out the biggest tree on the street.

"What do you notice about that tree?" she asked.

"It's the biggest," he said.

She nodded. "It seems that way. Because of our perspective. But as we drove here, I noticed that tree back there." She pointed to a tree at least three hundred meters away, just before the street twisted and the rest of it went out of sight. "That tree was actually the biggest."

Theo turned his head to look at her.

"With my lens, I can choose the perspective of anyone who looks at the photographs I take."

"So, it's about control?" Theo asked.

"It's about having a voice," she said as she turned a knob on the top of the camera and then lifted it to take a quick shot of Theo.

"Like this one." She turned the screen on the camera so that Theo could see the picture she took. "You've got a half-grin and every hair is perfectly in place. No one would guess that we were here waiting to see if there is a threat on your life in the place where you just stood. If I would have shot the same thing ten minutes before, your jaw was tight and your eyes narrow as you assessed everything going on around you, including my well-being. The moment I click, this button captures exactly what I want it to."

Theo nodded. He'd never thought of photography in such beautiful terms. He wondered if he had a passion for anything like that.

"We got the all clear, sir," River, one of his bodyguards, said from the front seat.

"Then let's get back," Theo said, feeling much happier than he had in a long time.

He realized he'd made a huge mistake. Someone could very much fall deeper into like with just small talk.

Eleven

As they drove back from the ribbon cutting ceremony to the castle, Alex couldn't believe what she'd said to Theo about her life behind the lens. When he looked at her with his gorgeous blue eyes, she wanted to spill everything she'd ever thought or felt, and she pretty much had. Man, she'd almost blown her cover way too many times.

And then when he touched her, a stupid shoulder brush had her knees quivering. Her only saving grace had been moving away from him. She'd never opened up to anyone like that, and some of the thoughts she had about photography hadn't ever even been as clear to her as when she told Theo about them.

And he'd seemed to welcome them. No, it was more than that. He acted as if what she was saying mattered to him. He really wanted to know how she looked at the world.

She shook her head. It was stupid to dwell on those thoughts. She had her future and he had Elise. *Ugh.* Why did his girlfriend have to be Elise? She could have been happy for him if it were anyone else, but the more she got to know Theo, the more she didn't want him with a woman who had the capability to be an evil wench.

But he was a big boy and he had made his choice. It wasn't

up to Alex to save him. Just because she may have had a crush on him when she was younger, and he may have asked her parents' permission to court her, although the jury was still out on that, it wasn't enough of a history for them to be responsible to protect one another, right? And maybe Elise had changed. Alex laughed out loud at the thought.

"What's so funny?" Theo asked as he watched Alex. Since Elise had already returned to the castle, Alex was asked to sit in back with Theo so that two guards could be in the car with them on their way back, instead of the solo officer who had driven them there. Everyone was on high alert, even though the code green had been a false alarm. Apparently one of the donors had tried to sneak in a daughter who was a huge Prince Theo fan, and it had all been sorted out quickly.

Alex knew she couldn't tell him the truth about why she'd laughed, then she remembered a moment she would have laughed about anyway. "I'm just remembering when Daniel jumped in front of you to protect you from that group of ten-year-old girls, like he was guarding the Pope," Alex said, and her laughter doubled in intensity. The look on their poor faces...priceless.

"They were more like fifteen, and the guy was just trying to do his job," Theo defended, but his chuckle gave away that he too thought the moment was pretty hilarious.

ELISE WAS MISSING from dinner later that evening, the king was still in meetings, and since Emmalee and Alex were shooting the dinner instead of eating with the family, the table seemed pretty empty.

Alex was working hard to get an angle that had good light in the chandelier-lit room, along with making sure Emmalee wasn't in the background, when Queen Marla cleared her throat. "I've heard that Elise has gone home?" she asked, and Theo looked up from his plate to meet his mother's eyes.

Theo nodded as Seb said, "Alright! You finally got some...."

He was interrupted when Queen Marla cleared her throat and glared down the table at her third son.

"Gumption," Seb continued, causing Tristan and Elliot to laugh.

Queen Marla turned her glare to her other younger sons and they quieted.

"And dumped the boring chick," Seb finished.

Theo broke up with Elise?

Theo shook his head. "We didn't break up."

"Man, I thought you might have finally pulled that stick out of your...."

Queen Marla's ahem was loud enough to cause Alex to take a step back.

"I was going to say bottom," Seb said.

The queen looked at Seb with narrowed eyes. "There is nothing wrong with Elise, nor is there anything wrong with your brother wanting to date her. He doesn't have a stick anywhere it shouldn't be."

"Well, that's a ringing endorsement of the woman. She's mother approved," Elliot said with a wink.

Queen Marla huffed before turning her attention back to Theo. "So why is she gone?"

"She missed home?" Theo said with a shrug.

"You didn't ask her?" his mother asked.

"We decided it wasn't the best time to go public with our relationship. I'm not sure why she left."

The queen sighed loudly. "Men," Queen Marla said. "It will be a wonder if any of you get married."

"Don't worry, Mother. I'm not planning on getting married," Seb said.

"Normally I would argue on that point, but honestly, I

wouldn't saddle any poor woman with you," the queen said, and the other three brothers roared with laughter.

"Any woman would be so lucky," Seb muttered.

Alex was surprised Emmalee had stayed quiet through the entire conversation. It wasn't like the woman not to let her presence be known, but maybe she was embracing the gist of her job and the fact that they were there to work, not find Prince Charming.

She was also quite pleased with the shots she'd captured that evening. Seb's face when his mother insulted him, the queen's smile when she got her sons to laugh, Theo's eyes when he saw the wait staff bring out his favorite dessert.

"I'm only going to say this once, Theo," Queen Marla said. "Don't let this one get away. Or you may be left with someone like that Torre girl."

Alex was grateful there was a wall behind her when the queen mentioned her name since she tripped and it caught her before she fell flat on her butt. It was the only thing between her and making a complete fool of herself.

Holy moly, Queen Marla hated her. She'd thought the princes had been doing more joking around than telling the truth in the gym, but evidently, they hadn't exaggerated the queen's dislike for Alexandra. Alex wasn't sure she deserved the ire, but she was grateful she only found the prince attractive and didn't have any real ambition to gain the throne of Valdoria because it looked like Queen Marla would be an immovable stumbling block.

She thought she caught Theo watching her from the corner of his eye for the briefest of moments, but when she turned her attention to him, he was watching his mother and the conversation she was having with Elliot.

"Did Daniel give you tomorrow's schedule?" Theo asked Alex after the meal had been cleared and before he left the room for the evening.

Alex nodded as she pulled it from her pocket.

"I'm thinking I might skip the gym in the morning, so we can meet at breakfast instead?" Theo asked.

"Sure," Alex said as Theo turned away.

Alex remembered the gap in the schedule that had her curiosity burning and decided to try to get Theo to divulge his midday whereabouts one more time.

"You won't need me between eleven and one either?" Alex asked.

Theo shook his head.

"Are you sure?" Alex asked. "I have nothing else planned."

Smart one, Alex. Of course, you don't have anything else planned. Your whole day revolves around him every day.

"I'm sure," Theo said with a smile before walking out of the door his mother and Emmalee had just left through moments before.

"The mysterious two-hour block where Theo disappears is gnawing at your curiosity as well?" Seb asked as he sidled up next to Alex.

"Not gnawing, per se."

Seb laughed. "Might as well give it up, pretty photographer girl. I've been trying for the past year and nada."

"Have you followed him?" Alex asked.

"I don't care that much," Seb said, laughing once again and then leaving the room with his brothers.

Alex wondered what type of semi-weekly event the heir would keep to himself that even his brothers didn't know about. It was all so cloak and dagger. Exactly the type of stuff Alex loved to be a part of.

She was still lost in thought when she got to her bedroom and kicked off her shoes. It wasn't until she was right next to her bed that she noticed a sparkly silver dress and a bunny mask laying on her white duvet.

What the heck?

As she lifted the dress, she saw a piece of paper flutter back down to the bed.

Alex,

Can you keep a secret?

Alex felt the speed of her heart ramp up and her hands became slick with sweat immediately. Had someone found her out? Was she going to be blackmailed? She turned over the piece of paper and read, *"Then be ready for the party of your life."*

A party.

She let out a breath of relief before wondering what kind of party needed a sparkly dress and a bunny mask. Halloween was still a month away. Upon further inspection, Alex saw that the silver dress also had black fringe along it's edges and it looked like it would fit like a glove.

"Jewel," she said to herself, and in that moment she decided there was nowhere else she'd rather be that night than at Jewel's party.

"I take it we're going?" Jane said as she let herself into Alex's room.

"A knock would be nice," Alex said as she continued to stare at the gorgeous dress. Jane had become more like a sister than an employee over the past year with all the time they'd spent together. An annoying and demanding sister, but a sister nonetheless.

Alex looked over at Jane to see that she was wearing a mid-calf black dress that fell straight from shoulders to legs, a very non-Jane-like outfit. She raised an eyebrow as she took in the look.

"Normally I'd be against this kind of a thing," Jane said.

"Because it would be a blast," Alex retorted, knowing she was getting under Jane's skin but not able to help it. The woman needed to loosen up.

"Because it could be dangerous."

Alex rolled her eyes.

"It's my job to protect you," Jane said with an exasperated sigh.

"How many times have we come across a threat on my life?" Alex asked as she rubbed the sequins on her silver dress up and then down. Why was that so satisfying?

"There was the time with the bird...."

"A legitimate threat," Alex added when Jane started the story about the one time a bird almost dive-bombed her in a park. She'd been saved from a nugget of caca on her head; it hadn't been a life-threatening moment.

"Since I started guarding you?" Jane asked.

Alex nodded. She already knew the answer.

"One," Jane said.

"What?" Alex asked as her head popped up.

"Mando told me about a letter that was sent to the castle...."

Alex stopped listening and went back to moving the sequins. "I said legitimate. We get a dozen of those a year," Alex interrupted.

"Those are legitimate, Alex. Normal people like Alex Turner would not think receiving a dozen death threats a year was typical. Thus, you have a bodyguard. Me. Let me do my job," Jane said.

She had a valid point. "Fine," Alex said. "So, you're nixing tonight?" Alex was surprised by how disappointed she felt. It had been a long time since she'd been invited to a party, heck, when was the last time she'd made a friend? She'd assumed her life as Alex Turner wouldn't have the constraints Alexandra Torre had, but she couldn't escape who she truly was, ever.

"I said normally," Jane said.

"You did," Alex responded, her heart beginning to lift.

"But this smells strongly of Jewel, and I trust her. As long as I get to go along and we don't leave the castle grounds, I don't see why we can't go."

That sounded fair. Alex smiled. "You trust someone?"

"If you can't stop with the smart remarks, no one is going to the party."

"Yes, mom," Alex said and then quickly added when she saw Jane's grimace, "Last one! I swear."

Alex got ready in a record amount of time since her mask covered her entire head. She didn't even bother with her typical braid and let her hair fall over her shoulders.

The dress Jewel chose for Alex was even more spectacular when put on. Like Jane's, it fell to her mid-calves and had tiny capped sleeves. Unlike Jane's, the sparkle of her dress was sure to be seen in outer space, and every edge was trimmed with black tassels. Alex loved it.

She did a little shimmy in front of the mirror, she couldn't help it, the dress asked for it, when there was a loud knock on her door.

Jane slipped on her deer mask as Alex put on her bunny one, and Jane answered the door. When it opened, it revealed a woman in a cream and maroon dress with the most intricate beading Alex had seen since her sister-in-law's wedding dress. Even though her head was covered by a mouse mask, Alex knew the woman was Jewel.

"Jewel?" Jane asked.

"Sh!" Jewel whispered. "The night is supposed to be anonymous."

Alex was surprised by how easy it was to speak and hear under their giant animal heads. She wondered if they were specially designed. She wouldn't put it past Jewel.

Jewel took Alex and Jane by their elbows and led them in the direction opposite the elevator. Jane gave Alex a hand motion over Jewel's head, the woman couldn't have been much over the five-foot mark, that said she was on guard.

Jewel led them to the end of the hallway where she pressed a button and the wall opened to reveal another elevator. Then she pushed Alex and Jane in. For such a small person, she sure packed a punch.

"What's with all the secrecy?" Jane asked.

At the same time, Alex realized they were leaving the intern hallway with no one else and said gleefully, "Emmalee's not coming? I mean, that's too bad she couldn't make it."

Jewel laughed. "None of the other interns were invited. They seemed like they'd be above a party like this." Jewel lifted her mouse nose into the air to signify the snobbery of the other interns. "And," she turned to Jane, "anonymity is a great way to create entertainment."

Jane nodded once and Alex felt like a little kid who'd been told she really could go to the candy store. She had to agree with Jewel, anonymity was making the anticipation factor on the party hit at least a level ten.

"So where are we going?" Jane asked.

"Here," Jewel said as the elevator doors opened and revealed the night sky.

Jane and Alex followed Jewel out and they stepped into a 1920's speakeasy. A gorgeous mahogany bar created a wall about thirty feet from the elevator and big brown leather couches sat around the makeshift room. Twinkle lights covered every surface and were strung between poles to make the whole portion of the rooftop feel lit, but mysterious. Huge pieces of red velvet fabric were hung between the same poles, creating temporary walls in the otherwise open space. Candles sat on coffee tables that matched the bar, and on the far end of the roof, a group of men in tuxes and, of course, animal heads played on saxophones, trumpets, and a piano.

"This is incredible," Alex said as Jane whistled.

"The decor is all Charlie," Jewel said, before she added, "Oops. I'm so not good at this secret thing. That's more Charlie's deal. I'm in it for the clothes." Jewel swiped a hand up and down the length of her body.

Alex could only imagine. She hadn't seen a better dressed group...ever. Every man was in a tux and every woman wore a dress that rivaled Alex's and Jane's. Jewel's dress was in a league of her own.

"You got the newbies to come," a deep voice said, causing the three women to turn away from the band and back toward the bar.

"I can't introduce you, right?" Jewel asked.

"We've been doing this for six months now. Do you really need to ask that question?" the man in the zebra head said.

"There will be plenty of anonymous faces in the crowd for them. They need to have a few friends in the mix," Jewel said.

"Fine. Tell them. Just make sure to play dumb in front of Charlie," the man said.

Jane and Alex nodded, but weren't sure they could keep their promise since they had no idea who Charlie was.

"She'll be the only person Jewel won't introduce you to," the man added.

Ah, that made sense.

"I'm Reggie. Charlie's boyfriend and, therefore, co-conspirator in these parties," Reggie said with an outstretched hand.

Alex felt callouses on his big hands and figured he must use them a lot in whatever his line of work might be. She wondered if maybe he was behind the beautiful bar and coffee tables.

"What are these parties?" Jane asked.

"Charlie is obsessed with a cancelled television program that had a few episodes with a secret group that held parties like this. We had a need for some kind of entertainment since there's a large group of us twenty-somethings that wanted to have a good time but didn't want to go into town to the local pub where the older, married guys hang out," Reggie said.

"The guys are gross. They hit on anything with two legs," Jewel added.

"So, she had us pool our skills. I'm the muscle, Jewel's the dresser, and Charlie's behind the design. Charlie does decorating in the castle and the queen gives her pretty much leeway. Whenever items of furniture aren't in use, Charlie can use them for parties."

"That's nice of the queen," Alex said.

Reggie shrugged. "It's the least she could do since her sons tend to crash every one of these they can."

"He's not a big fan of the princes?" Alex whispered to Jewel.

"Charlie's got a crush on our fair prince and Tristan likes to flirt. A lot. And he's flirted one too many times with Charlie," Jewel whispered back.

"Speaking of the devils," Reggie said.

The elevator doors had opened and three men in suits, all in lion heads, strutted into the party. Even though every man in the room was wearing a tuxedo and it should have, by all means, been a better look than an average suit, that wasn't the case. These suits fit each of the princes like they were born in them, molded to their broad shoulders and defined muscles, and something about their slightly more casual look made them stick out. Not that they wouldn't stick out anyway; there was nothing average about the Valdorian princes.

Conversations stopped and each and every female head turned toward the princes almost as if they had no choice. They reeked of charisma and captured attention like warriors.

Reggie shook his head before walking away, Alex presumed to find and stake his claim on his girlfriend.

"That's Seb and Tristan for sure, but is it Elliot or Theo with them?" a woman in a fish mask said as she slid to a stop beside Jewel.

"Alex and Jane, this loudmouth is Danielle," Jewel introduced.

"I just said what you were thinking. I'm going to go around and take bets. You guys want in on the action?" Danielle asked.

"On which of the princes is here tonight?" Jane asked.

Alex looked the men over and knew in an instant that the man leading the group was Theo. The way he held his shoulders and the sureness of his step was without a doubt the crown prince. She wouldn't have known the other two were Seb and Tristan, but she knew Theo.

She was stunned by the revelation. What did that mean? Her breath quickened with the implications of her discovery. Was she obsessed with him, the same way every other woman in the world was?

No. She took his picture every day. Of course she knew his mannerisms. It had nothing to do with what she felt. It had everything to do with her job. She drew in another breath more slowly, this time to relax.

"Yeah," Danielle said.

Alex shook her head as the other women in her group did the same. No amount of money was worth drawing attention to the fact that she knew Theo was there that night. She liked that he didn't know she was there and that he didn't know she knew who he was. There was definitely something interesting about this whole anonymous thing.

"Your loss," Danielle said as she walked away and a woman with a gorilla mask took her place.

"The clothing is spot on, as always," Gorilla mask said.

"As is the decor," Jewel said.

Ah, gorilla mask was Charlie.

"Did Reggie find you?" Jewel asked.

"Is he looking for me?" Charlie feigned innocence. "I may have switched masks with Liz about half an hour ago. What fun is an anonymous party if your boyfriend knows what you're wearing?"

Charlie walked away as Jewel said under breath, "That isn't going to end well."

"Where did you find all of these clothes?" Alex asked as she took in dress after dress. They were perfect. And not just with the theme, but they perfectly fit the women who wore them.

"I made them," Jewel said before walking toward the bar.

"You what?" Alex asked. There had to be thirty dresses in the room.

"Fashion isn't just my job, it's my hobby. Most of these are vintage pieces I found that I did a few alterations on to make them fit the wearer. But a few, like yours and mine, are custom Jewel creations," Jewel said.

"You're like the Annie Leibowitz of fashion," Alex said in awe.

"Who?" Jewel asked.

"She may know everything about fashion, but that keeps her from knowing much about anything else," a teasing voice said as a lion-headed-suit-wearing-prince joined the group and sidled up next to Jewel.

Jewel moved away from the prince but not before landing a well-placed elbow in his side.

"Ouch," the prince said. "For someone so small, you sure can land a jab."

"Are you lost, Tristan?" Jewel asked.

Tristan, of course. Tristan's voice was a tiny bit deeper than any of the other brothers.

"I think your admirers have gathered in a group over there." Jewel pointed to a group of women seated on the couch nearest the bar that all had their animal heads turned toward Tristan.

"They don't know who I am," Tristan said quietly before adding, "this is all anonymous, remember?"

"You couldn't hide that huge ego of yours in a dozen lion heads," Jewel said, and Alex laughed. The girl was quick.

Tristan clutched his chest. "First, fine maiden, you wound my physical being and then you wound my spirit. What is a man to do?"

"Leave?" Jewel said.

"As you wish," Tristan said with one last look at Jewel before walking to the sofa with his admirers.

"What was that?" Alex asked.

"Let's go get a drink," Jewel said and pounded her hand on the bar to get the attention of the hyena serving drinks.

Alex knew deflection when she saw it, and Jewel was deflecting hard. There was definitely something going on between Jewel and Tristan, but Alex wasn't one to judge when it came to keeping secrets. Except when it came to Theo's. What was it about his that made her want to dig like a rabbit before winter?

"I want a special," Jewel said to the bartender. "What about you guys?" She turned to Alex and Jane.

"I'm not a big drinker," Jane said. Alex knew she'd never drink on duty, and while she was with Alex, she was always on duty.

"Neither am I," Alex said. She hadn't touched the stuff in her life. It had been a drunk driver who'd killed her big sister, and she'd never been tempted to partake.

"You're in luck. The special is always a virgin drink," Jewel said. "I'm not a fan of the hard stuff, either. We'll take three specials," she said to the bartender.

The women got their drinks and then headed toward a couch and coffee table space that had yet to be occupied. There were five sitting areas, and most of the people were crowded at the two the Valdorian princes had decided to sit. A few stragglers, all men, sat at the space nearest the band. It seemed there wasn't a single female in the room who could stay away from the princes.

"Is this how all the parties go?" Jane asked Jewel.

"All the fun stops when the princes show up," Jewel said as she flung her hand in the air. "Why do they even come? These things are supposed to be for their employees. Or at least they were until the princes started showing up, and then other nobles followed suit and crashed our parties. But the attendees are mainly the help. Don't they know everyone gets bummed out when the bosses show up?"

No one looked anywhere near bummed that the princes had shown, but Alex and Jane let Jewel continue her rant.

"Isn't it enough that they have every woman outside of the castle fawning over them? They have to make sure every woman inside of the castle, all of my friends, are in love with them too? The only saving grace is they only come when they're on leave. Stupid anniversary party has them all home at once."

Alex and Jane exchanged a look, and even behind their masks they knew what the other was saying. Jewel was not a fan of the Valdorian princes, putting it mildly.

"Do you know them very well?" Alex asked.

"You mean the princes?" Jewel said.

Alex nodded.

Jewel shrugged. "I was raised on the castle grounds. My parents both worked here. My mom in housekeeping and my dad as a groundskeeper. Mom likes to think of the princes as her unofficial sons. She worked in the nursery for the years when the princes were young. I grew up in a little cottage that way." Jewel pointed off the roof toward the west. "There are a bunch of homes for the married castle staff. Most of the unmarrieds, like me, live right under where we're standing." Jewel pointed to the floor. "So, I guess I know them well enough. I used to play with them when we were kids and all on the same level, but we became teenagers and... let's just say things changed. Now these parties are basically the only time we see them or any of the other nobles' kids."

Alex nodded. She knew what royal life was like. As kids, they were encouraged to spend time with any and everyone, but then as they grew up, they were supposed to tighten their circle and be smart about those they let in. Alex wished she'd been smarter.

"So, I don't know them in the way you do. Royals and royals," Jewel said, and then she popped a hand over her mouse mouth.

"What do you mean by that?" Jane asked. Alex would have spoken, but all ability to function had gone out the window. Jewel knew.

"Oh, dang it," Jewel said, her mouth still covered with her hand. "I'm so bad at secrets," she said, dropping her hand. "I didn't want you to know I knew. I figured the secret must be important if you were trying to hide your identity."

Jewel lifted her mask slightly in order to chug down half of her drink.

"I'm not hiding my identity," Jane finally said since Alex was still frozen.

"Yes, you are," Jewel said as she took some peanuts from a dish on the table and shoved them under her mask. "But the identity that is more important to hide is yours, right?" Jewel looked at Alex.

"How did you know?" Alex asked. There was no use in denying it. Jewel was sure she was right.

"I've wanted to be a royal tailor since I was six. I studied every royal family in the world in case I didn't get the position here. I've known your measurements since you were fifteen. There was no way you could walk into a crowded ballroom without me knowing, much less have one on one time together. And you," she turned to Jane, "have bodyguard written all over your demeanor. You squint more than you smile, and you walk with such rigid posture I want to throw a spider on you just to see you curl up in some way."

"I'm not afraid of spiders," Jane said.

"Of course you aren't," Jewel replied.

Alex felt her throat closing at the thought of anyone else knowing about her secret. "You can't tell anyone who I am. Does anyone else know?"

Jewel shook her head. "Not that I've heard, and I'm pretty clued in on the gossip in this place. And I wasn't planning on saying anything, but you've seen how good I am at secrets."

"Please." Alex begged. She hated having any loose ends, especially loose ends she couldn't control. "Imagine if your job was on the line, your dream?"

Jewel sat still for a moment before nodding and then said, "You have my word."

Alex believed that Jewel would somehow manage to keep her secret, and she let out a breath, feeling a bit lightheaded.

"Thank you," Alex said.

"Jewel," Charlie said as she scurried up to the group. "What are you guys doing all alone over here? Never mind. I don't have time to hear your answer. Jewel, I need your help with my special project."

"No," Jewel groaned as she leaned back on the couch. "You can't seriously be thinking about doing it still."

"Of course we're doing it. Tonight is the six-month anniversary of our parties. We need to celebrate."

"By dying?" Jewel asked.

"No one is going to die," Charlie said, and from her tone, Alex knew there had to be rolling eyes happening behind her mask.

Charlie walked away as Jewel turned to Alex and Jane. "I have to help her. If I don't, people really may get hurt."

"That sounds ominous," Jane said.

"Because it is. I better go," Jewel said as she got up and followed the way Charlie had gone.

Alex was quite curious about what Charlie had planned and figured she'd find out in the very near future.

As she watched Jewel go, she tried not to dwell on the fact that she'd have to trust a woman she met only a few days before to keep a secret that could change her entire life. Alex knew if she continued sitting there she'd just stew about Jewel knowing her truth. But there was nothing she could do now, so she sought for distraction somewhere, anywhere.

"We should probably go mingle," Alex said as she looked around the party and realized they stuck out like sore thumbs. Mingling could help her to forget and keep anyone else from guessing her identity, even if it was just her Alex Turner one. She liked being anonymous. Win, win.

Jane nodded.

They started to walk toward the group congregated closest to them when Alex stopped. "It's kind of fun that no one here knows us. If we show up at a group together we're sure to stick out. Want to divide and conquer?" Alex asked.

"Sure," Jane said with a shrug of her shoulders before she continued walking to the group they were going to join, and Alex left to go to the other group.

There weren't any open seats when Alex got to the group of couches she'd assigned herself, so she leaned against the arm of one of them and tried to inconspicuously join the conversation. Well not join as much as eavesdrop.

"I would love to go to the Sahara," a girl with a perfect manicure, obviously a noble, said with a sigh. Alex didn't like to be harsh on her own sex, but she had to imagine that manicure and the girl accompanying it wouldn't last too long in the desert. Heck, Alex knew she wouldn't.

"The accommodations weren't exactly five star." Since she knew the voice that came from the lion head wasn't Tristan's nor Theo's, Alex figured out it was Seb.

"I don't need five stars. Four would be just fine," the girl joked, and Alex laughed along with the group. At least manicure knew she wouldn't cut it.

Of course the conversation at these parties would be about the princes. Alex wondered what kind of stories Tristan was telling. Judging from Jane's hunched shoulders, they were pretty funny.

She went from watching Jane to continuing to listen to stories about Seb and Theo. Seb was the main storyteller and also the hero in most of the tales. She stopped listening after a while and thought about leaving the party, but then she remembered why Jewel had left. Her curiosity wouldn't let her go without knowing what Charlie had planned.

"Why do you have to serve in the military anyway? It stinks that you guys are gone so much of the year," a woman in a seal mask asked loudly enough that it brought Alex's attention back to the conversation next to her.

Her first thought on the masks was spot on. The masks *had* to be specially made. There were so many different kinds and, somehow, they kept the wearer hidden while allowing easy access to food and drink and not hindering conversation in the least. It seemed like the type of task totally up Jewel's alley.

"We serve our country in any way it needs us," Seb said in a responsible tone that was unlike the man that Alex had come to know. Maybe the guy wasn't all about flirting and joking.

"Even Theo?" Seal mask asked. She didn't look at any specific lion head, so Alex was pretty sure she had no idea which of the princes was sitting in the area with her.

"Especially Theo," Seb answered. "Theo did his five years and came out a war hero, and now he'll serve us all as king."

Theo was a lot more complex than he first appeared.

"War hero, really?" Theo said, sounding a bit strange.

"The guy barely survived basic training," Theo said in the weird way again, and Alex realized what he was doing. He was doing an impression of Elliot. The relaxed way he held onto the last syllables of his words wasn't like Theo at all. He was trying to hide in plain sight.

The group laughed and Alex joined them. She was laughing more at Theo's hiding than at his joke.

"He came up with a strategy for peace with a country that

will remain nameless but has been a thorn in our side for years. Hero isn't a strong enough term," Seb said.

Alex cocked her head in approval. If what Seb said was true, she had to agree with the title Seb had bestowed on Theo. She knew from the strategy meetings she'd sat through that coming up with terms of peace accords was one of the most difficult things a monarch faced. Theo had brains too.

She closed her eyes behind her mask, annoyed as her crush grew.

But how could she help it? The guy was indisputably the most beautiful being on the planet with his aquamarine eyes and full lips. Alex never craved the ocean until she saw Theo's eyes on a daily basis. His jawline and even the planes of his shoulders were cut as if created with an artist's knife. And don't get her started on seeing him with his shirt off. And then on top of that he was kind, smart, funny, and sweet. She needed to stop thinking about him.

"Really?" Manicure girl asked, looking from Seb to Theo.

"I'd love to divulge more details, sweetheart. But if I did, I'd have to kill you," Seb said, and manicure girl giggled.

Theo shook his head so slightly that Alex almost didn't catch it. He was giving Seb some kind of sign, but Seb looked away without acknowledging Theo.

"Theo really is the best of us brothers," Seb said.

A lightbulb lit in Alex's mind, and she realized Seb was trying to talk up Theo. Seb was obviously bored with Elise, he'd said as much himself, and with the girl gone, he saw tonight as a way to put another girl in Theo's arms. Or at least get Elise out of them. Alex felt a fire kindling in her chest and hated to admit what emotion was causing that fire. She couldn't be jealous; what she felt for Theo was a crush. Crushes were meaningless.

But how was Seb going to push some unsuspecting girl at Theo if Theo wasn't even willing to divulge his true identity.

Maybe Seb assumed Theo would be more willing to find a new girl if he were disguised as Elliot? That didn't seem likely.

Alex's musings were cut short when Theo stood and mumbled an apology before leaving the group. As he passed Alex, he linked his arm through hers and she had no choice but to follow him as they walked toward the band.

"What are you doing?" Alex sputtered as soon as they were out of earshot of anyone in the room. Here she had been just pining after the man and now he was touching her? It was doing all kinds of things to her already haggard emotions.

"I'm Theo," Theo said as if that answered her question.

"Okay, but what are you doing?" she asked again.

Theo looked from her to the group he'd left.

"I needed a break from my brother and a girl on my arm to do it. You're the only woman in the room I want to spend time with, so...."

"And you didn't think to ask me if I wanted to spend time with you?" Of all the cocky, assuming men... "Wait, how did you know who I was?"

Twelve

She was right. He'd assumed she wouldn't mind because no woman ever minded spending time with him, but Alex was different. The reason he wanted to spend time with her was the same reason she might not want to be with him.

"I'm sorry. I'm here hiding as Elliot because this party isn't the kind of thing Prince Theo Kane should attend, and Seb is about to blow my cover out of the water so that he can..." Theo paused, not wanting to tell Alex what Seb thought Theo should do now that Elise was out of town. "Do you mind being a diversion so that my brother quits embarrassing me, him, and the rest of the Kanes?" he said instead.

Alex pulled her body back from Theo and he had to let go of her arm. "No, I guess I don't." She surprised him with her answer. "And how did you know who I was?"

That was easy, but Theo couldn't give her the truth. He would have been able to spot her in a dark room with only a candle to guide him. He'd gotten to know her voice, her scent, her silhouette. Every part of her was engraved in his mind.

"Jane has a very distinct walk, and it wasn't a flying leap to figure you were the woman with her. I like your dress, by the way."

Alex paused and he hoped he made her blush with his compliment, but the stupid bunny mask wasn't doing him any favors.

"Thanks," she said before turning away and leading him toward the end of the bar that had a few vacant stools. "Do you mind if I eat some peanuts while we hide away from your brother. I'm starving," she said as she motioned to the open stool beside her.

As Theo sat on the stool, he realized Alex had just walked in front of him and directed him on what he should do. Theo was trying to remember the last time a person had led him anywhere. He didn't mean to always be the one to take charge, but it was a part of who he was. He was surprised by how much he liked watching Alex do the leading. She thought of him as her equal and he appreciated that. People tended to put him on a pedestal, and he was bound to fall from the high seat.

He then remembered that Daniel also led him places, but he only led him to where Theo had already appointed he wanted to be. Speaking of his assistant, where was the guy? Theo had only come tonight because Daniel had asked for him to be a wingman with a girl he was really into. Scratch that. That wasn't the only reason. A small, stupid part of him had hoped Alex would be here. He really wanted to see the woman outside of her work environment. He knew it was a long shot since the interns weren't technically castle staff, nor were they nobles like the other partygoers, but as soon as he'd walked in, he had noticed her standing with the other two women. Even with the stupid mask on she was like a lighthouse beckoning to him.

Fool. She's a friend. If that.

Too bad Daniel wasn't beckoning as loudly. Theo wanted to get his task done with and leave. Seeing Alex outside of a work environment was a bad idea.

But here he was. With her. Because he'd commandeered her.

"Is this your kind of scene?" she asked as she shoveled a few mixed nuts under her mask. That seemed like it could be a loaded question and Theo wished he could see her eyes. Those bright green features were easier to read than any book.

"Not really," he said without thinking.

"Let me guess. You'd rather be reading or working out." Alex laughed.

"No. I can have fun." Theo wasn't sure why he felt so defensive. He only knew he didn't want her to think he was boring as she assumed he was.

"But you just said this wasn't your scene."

Dang it, he had. But with his reputation on the line, Theo needed to fight. She thought she had him all pegged. A dull heir with nothing on his mind but work.

"I meant this particular spot. These parties change location every week."

"Uh huh."

Why wasn't Alex more gullible?

"I like to have a good time," Theo said, pushing harder. He did. He'd dated dozens of women and traveled the globe. He'd been to red carpet events on almost every continent. Not that he enjoyed many of those events, but he'd done them and should get credit.

"With a book."

The woman didn't give up, and if he was being completely honest, she was right. This scene was definitely the type of situation his brothers and even Daniel sought out. He would always choose a small event with people he cared about over a huge party with tons of strangers. Knowing he'd lost this battle, he decided to turn the tables.

"Are you some kind of party animal?" Theo asked, groaning in defeat.

"Nope," Alex said, and Theo knew she was grinning under her mask. "But like you, I like to have a good time."

She was mocking him, and Theo couldn't help but chuckle. Especially because he knew he'd get her back in a few minutes.

"Okay, in all seriousness. What is the perfect night in Prince Theo Kane's book?" Alex asked.

He raised his eyebrows even though he knew she couldn't see them. He'd been thrown by her personal question. Typically, she kept to her stuff and he kept to his. But maybe today's event had bonded them, or maybe the wall she was trying to keep him behind was crumbling. He was annoyed by how much that thought cheered him.

Theo cocked his head as he thought. He remembered the cheesy answer he'd given *Celebrity Magazine* when they featured him. Ugh, just thinking about the article made his stomach turn. He was just about to say the generic *walking on a moonlit beach* when something honest in him stopped those words from coming out and instead he said, "The what doesn't matter as much as the who it's with."

Alex sat up straighter and he knew she was studying him, but before she could respond or he could reciprocate the question, Charlie stopped the music.

"As you all know, we've been throwing these parties for six months," she said into a microphone.

The rooftop erupted into cheering. "So, to celebrate...." She paused. "You know what? It's easier to show you than to tell you. Follow me."

The entire party began to move toward the elevator, but Theo knew a way to bypass the crowd. Caught up in the moment, he grabbed Alex's hand and ran toward the staircase that would take them from the roof to any floor of the castle. Theo loved the feel of her small hand in his, but told himself he wasn't holding her hand for his enjoyment. He only wanted her close so that he could see how she would react to Charlie's surprise. He knew she'd flip, and he'd have a bit of vengeance for the way she'd teased him about his monotonous life.

No one else at the party knew what was happening. He only knew because when Charlie had ran it past his mom, he'd overheard the conversation. Lucky for Charlie, his mom was a fan of the same show Charlie was obsessed with, and recreating that scene was something that would, to quote the queen, "please me greatly." So she gave Charlie permission.

"Are you afraid of heights?" Theo asked as they ran down the steps in front of the other partygoers who decided to bypass the line. They'd stopped on a landing for a brief moment for Alex to take off her shoes, but it was long enough for others to begin to catch up to them. They were still in front of the crowd, but footsteps were just meters behind their own. He picked up their pace and the six flights down didn't seem bad at all. He was pleasantly surprised that Alex had kept up with him.

The excitement of the group continued to grow as they left the castle. The farther they got from the rooftop and the closer they got to their final destination, the more the anticipation became almost palpable. 'Lifers', or the kids of staff and nobles who had grown up on the castle grounds now began to realize where they were going. A few became a bit wary, but for most of them the anticipation only increased.

The lush green grass of the castle grounds gave way to more rocky and thorny terrain. It wasn't until Alex began to slow down that Theo realized what the ground must be doing to her feet. Without thought, he swept her up into his arms and continued with the rest of the group.

"What are you doing?" Alex said in a whisper that only he could hear.

"Weren't your feet hurting?" Theo asked.

"Yes. But what will people say?" Alex turned from left to right to see if anyone had stopped to gawk at them.

Theo didn't feel the slightest bit of concern, which wasn't like him at all. He'd always lived with an internal fear of what his actions could do to taint Valdoria, the crown, and the Kane family. It was actually the only fear he had in life. But the freedom the masks gave was invigorating. He felt like he could do anything. He was literally fearless, and right now he wanted to save Alex's feet from unneeded torture.

"No one knows which Kane I am. They'll assume I'm Elliot, Tristan, or worst, Seb. None of them would think twice about carrying a girl in their arms."

"But you're not," Alex said, more quietly than she'd been speaking before.

Theo didn't need the reminder that his life was fraught with responsibility and duty that his brothers never needed to worry about. But tonight, he didn't have to either.

"Let me be the dashing prince that saves the princess just for tonight," Theo said.

He felt Alex's entire body tighten and go rigid in his arms. "I'm not a princess."

He was again reminded that he needed to find out what Alex's deal was. Why was she hiding her true identity and why was it so imperative that her identity stay a mystery? The only times he'd ever witnessed her nervous or anxious was when her secret was in jeopardy.

"But tonight, you can be," he said.

Her body went lax in his arms, and she even lifted one of her own to wrap around Theo's neck. Theo wouldn't let himself think about how perfectly she fit with her head on his chest and legs draped over his arm. The night was cool, but Theo felt himself get hotter and hotter as his thoughts betrayed him and thought about the woman in his arms.

"No!" he heard someone shout as they got to the old palace grounds.

Alex dropped her arm from around his shoulders and he knew it was time to let her down, which he did so, regretfully. He wondered if he'd ever experience holding her close again.

Imbecile. She's not yours. Nor had she been, nor would she ever be.

Maybe he'd only enjoyed the moment because he was living out a situation that a former Theo would have died for a chance at. Or maybe, most likely, he was only fooling himself.

He shook his head, trying to rid it of thoughts about the beautiful woman at his side, and looked up at the dilapidated wall in front of him. The castle he and his family resided in was built in the late fifteen hundreds. However, the royal family had occupied the space in front of him for thousands of years before that. But when the "new" castle had been built, the old palace had been left to ruin. He, his brothers, and many of the 'lifers' had used the grounds as the best childhood fort, but he was pretty sure no one else had set foot there in years, if not decades.

Someone had begun handing out umbrellas as a male voice said, "Charlie, just because Rory survived doesn't mean we will too. Have you even measured how high the top of the wall is?"

"Of course. Have a little faith in me," Charlie said as she handed Theo and Alex umbrellas.

"I've seen that episode. This is insane," Alex said as she backed up a few steps.

"I thought you were always up for a good time," Theo teased, feeling a bit braver now that Alex wasn't keen on the idea.

But as he looked up at the wall, the saner part of him realized Alex was right. His mother would have never approved if she'd known the height of the wall Charlie had chosen. Theo figured the top of it was probably about two and a half stories up. On one side of the wall was a rope ladder that someone, he was assuming Charlie, had somehow rigged up. The grass and brambles around the base of the wall would soften anyone's fall, but he had to wonder if the umbrella would do anything. Theo also took a step backwards.

"You want us to jump off of that thing?" someone asked.

"In solidarity. We're kind of a secret society," Charlie said.

"Nope. We just work together," another voice said.

"Lots of us don't even work with you." Theo identified the voice of Christian, one of his advisors' sons, call out.

"But these parties, the masks." Charlie's voice became strained like she was fighting tears. This obviously meant a lot to her.

One of the lion masked men, who Theo recognized as Tristan, walked toward Charlie and looped an arm around her shoulders. "It really could end tragically, love," Tristan said.

"But it could be awesome," Charlie said before shaking Tristan's arm off and climbing the rope ladder with an umbrella under her arm.

"Charlie," a woman in a mouse mask ran toward the bottom of the ladder and grabbed ahold of Charlie's foot. "It really doesn't seem safe."

"I'm going to do it. And you'll all see that it is safe and then we can all jump. In solidarity."

"We all love you and love the parties and spending time together, isn't that enough?" Mouse mask asked.

Charlie shook mouse mask's hand off of her foot and began climbing again.

"She's really going to do it," Alex said, looking up at Theo with her infuriating mask on. He had no idea what she was thinking other than that her voice held a tiny tremble.

"Don't do it, Charlie," another woman called out and then began to sob. Things were going downhill fast. Theo felt a responsibility to do something, but he had no idea what. He looked around the group and then at the surrounding area, hoping something would come to him.

The first man that had talked about how high the wall was began to climb up after Charlie. "You can't do this, Char," he said as he followed her up the ladder. "We can find another way to join together in solidarity."

What was it with this girl and solidarity?

"You and Jewel are 'lifers', you wouldn't understand," Charlie said as she reached the top. The wind in the area had begun to pick up and Alex wrapped her arms around herself. Theo absent-mindedly took off his jacket and wrapped it around her shoulders, then moved to where his brothers stood.

"We have to stop this," Theo said to Tristan and Seb.

"How?" Tristan asked. "I tried."

"Is there any way to catch her if she does jump?" Seb asked.

Brilliant. He should have come to his brothers sooner. As Theo looked around the group, he noticed a girl wearing a blanket around her shoulders.

"That could work," Theo said as he pointed to the woman.

Tristan nodded, walked over to the woman and came back with the blanket.

"Now what do we do?" Tristan asked. "Stand under the wall like some firemen and hope that flimsy thing holds up?"

"Do you have a better idea?" Theo asked.

Tristan shook his head and followed as the other two walked to right under where Charlie stood. By this time, the man that had followed her had also made it to the top of the wall.

"What are you guys doing?" Charlie called down to the princes.

"Just hanging out," Tristan said as he threw one end of the blanket to Theo and Seb held another corner. A masked man came out of the group to take the last corner.

"I don't need that. I've done the research. This is going to work," Charlie said.

"The show isn't exactly scientific evidence," the man on the wall said.

"It's going to work," Charlie said stubbornly as she opened her umbrella.

Theo willed his brain to come up with a solution and thought about Charlie's motivation. If she wanted solidarity, she'd hate to lose further parties. Theo finally had an answer better than the stupid blanket he was holding.

"The queen won't be happy on the off chance someone gets hurt," Theo called up.

"What?" Charlie asked. "I cleared it with her earlier."

"Does she know how high this wall is?" Theo asked. He couldn't see Charlie well but thought he saw her shaking her head.

"What do you think she'll do if someone gets hurt? Maybe this is as safe as jumping off of a forty-foot wall could be, but is it worth losing all future parties?" Theo went in for the kill.

No words came from the top of the wall and Theo wished he were closer to Charlie so that he could shake some sense into her. She'd always seemed like a pleasant and bright person, but this moment defied what he once thought he knew.

"No," she finally said. "Fine, I'll come...."

Charlie didn't finish what she was saying as an enormous gust of wind, that Theo felt even standing right beside the wall, blew through.

"Ahhhh!" she screamed, and a body came flying down the side of the wall.

Theo and his brothers moved to catch it, but the body that fell wasn't the one they'd been expecting. It was the man that had been up there with Charlie.

The extra weight and the suddenness of the fall kept them from getting a good position or grip on the blanket, and instead of catching the man, the blanket was ripped out of Seb's and Tristan's hands and the man fell to the brush beneath.

All four men holding the blanket swore as they dropped to their knees and tried to help the man moaning on the ground.

"I called emergency services," a voice behind them yelled, and Theo heard screams and cries in the background but focused on the man on the ground.

"Don't move him," Alex's voice commanded as the last man

who'd held the blanket reached for the fallen man's mask. "We don't know what kind of injuries he could have incurred, and he could have hurt his spine."

"What did I do?" Theo heard Charlie call out, but he pushed her noise to the background.

"What should we do?" Theo looked up to Alex. She seemed to be the only one keeping a cool head.

"How far out is emergency services?" Alex asked.

"Two minutes," came the reply.

"Reggie?" Alex asked as she knelt beside Theo. "Where does it hurt?"

"Everywhere," Reggie moaned.

"He's speaking. That's good," Alex said, turning to Theo for a second before looking back at Reggie.

"Can you move your arms?" she asked.

Theo saw one of Reggie's fingers twitch.

"That's good," Alex said, but Theo heard the strain in her voice.

Soon flashing lights were followed by the wail of a siren. Theo got up and began to clear a path through the spectators. Alex ran behind him to help keep people out of the way.

The paramedics sped through the crowd and asked Reggie a few questions before lifting him onto their stretcher.

"I'm so sorry," Charlie wailed as mouse mask girl held her. Charlie tried to pull away. "I want to ride in the ambulance with him."

"We'll follow in my car," Mouse mask said, and the two women ran back toward the castle. Nearly half the group did the same.

"I'll be the family representative," Seb offered before jumping into the ambulance, and the emergency vehicle peeled away.

The rest of the stragglers walked slowly back to the castle.

Theo looked over at Alex and noticed she'd taken her mask off. He did the same.

"You kept quite the cool head," he said, not able to help himself as he took her in from head to toe. She was the most gorgeous woman he'd ever seen, and tonight she was even more. That kind of calm couldn't be learned, and it was exactly what any person in a high-profile position needed.

She threw her head upside down and pulled all of her hair on top of her head as she tied it in a knot.

"I could say the same for you. You kept Charlie from jumping."

"A lot of good that did," Theo muttered. "What happened up there anyway?"

"You didn't see it?" Alex asked. She looked drained as she held her limp mask in one hand and her heels in the other.

Theo pointed to his own stupid mask.

"And it probably didn't help that you were right against the base of the wall. Charlie's umbrella got caught up in that gust of wind, and she was already so close to the edge. She teetered and Reggie pulled her back, but that threw him off balance and he ended up going over instead. He saved her." Alex looked down at her feet for a second before looking at Theo and then up at where Reggie had fallen from. Was she likening Theo's carrying her across the thorns to what Reggie'd done? No. That was wishful thinking.

But she had moved her gaze back to him, and he was finally getting to look into her soulful eyes that always spoke to him, whether he wanted them to or not. The look of admiration in them changed to trepidation.

"He's going to be alright, isn't he?" she asked.

Theo realized Alex hadn't heard what the paramedics had said on site, since she was busy comforting Charlie before she left for the hospital. "He'll be fine. Eventually. A few broken bones at worst. He got lucky."

Alex nodded as the tension that had been sitting above her eyes disappeared.

"I guess we better get back," Theo said as he lifted Alex once again. He hadn't even thought about it; his body had just done it even as his mind told him to create some space between them.

"I can walk," Alex said, and Theo felt her body stiffen. But even that didn't stop him.

"I know." They'd already had this discussion before, and he wasn't about to get into an argument that he could possibly lose. What he was doing wasn't smart, but it didn't stop him from wanting to do it. Better to agree with her and get his dumb way.

"You already carried me here. What about...?" Her voice trailed off.

"There's no one left to see us."

He felt her body relax into his as she wrapped her arm around his neck, and Theo felt immediate guilt that his first thought was being grateful that the night's events had landed Alex in his arms once again.

Thirteen

Having Theo carry her was driving her all kinds of insane. It had been crazy enough when he grabbed her hand as they ran, but this was too much for her poor crush-affected emotions to handle. She needed to think about anything other than the hardness of his muscles pressing against her back.

"It probably wasn't the smartest thing for us to follow the crowd like that," Alex said, realizing it probably sounded like she was admonishing Theo, which she wasn't. She knew what the responsibilities of the future crown could do to a man, and she was glad he'd found time for fun. It was part of the reason why she'd teased him about his lack of partying earlier. She'd hoped it would spur him on in his adventure seeking behavior that night. "I mean for me," she added. "I could have lost my chance at the job with Jacques."

She shuddered when she realized how possible it could have been. Maybe it still could be. News of Reggie was sure to get around, and if it got back to Jacques that she was in the mix, would he think she was too irresponsible for the job? Or maybe he'd even be annoyed that she hadn't caught the moment on film?

And then she remembered her mask. She'd had it on almost

the whole night. She had to hope it had been enough. It was too late to worry about it now.

There seemed to be a whole lot in her life she was pushing out of her mind and hoping for the best outcome. Her luck had to run out sometime. Hopefully it would hold out just long enough.

"Why is the job with Jacques so important?" Theo asked as he slowed his pace. Was she getting too heavy?

"You can put me...."

"You better not end that sentence with down. I'm fine."

Yeah, he was. And that was part of the problem.

"You didn't answer my question," Theo said.

Alex wasn't sure how much to share. Theo knew her family, and if she gave any details about her life before the internship, would he be tipped off? No. If he hadn't put two and two together by that point, she had nothing to worry about.

"My big sister was the one who fell in love with photography first. When we were all clamoring for the latest cell phones, she asked for a camera. I still remember the Christmas she got it, she hugged it to her chest and didn't let it go until mom made her come to breakfast." Alex smiled at the memory. Lizzie's reaction to the camera had been a scream that had to have startled everyone in the entire castle.

"She died a few years later." Alex decided not to tell Theo the horrible details of that tragic time, but by the way he tightened his grip on her, she wondered if he understood. So she found herself going on to tell him things she hadn't told anyone, not even her family - that Lizzie had been on her way to get shots of a sunflower field when the drunk driver killed her. Alex worried that in their grief, her parents would throw away the camera, and along with it, the memories of what Lizzie had treasured. Alex had to keep it. And though she'd long ago upgraded from that camera, she still took it with her everywhere she lived. It was like having a piece of Lizzie by her side.

"And you took up where she left off?" Theo asked quietly.

Alex nodded.

"I would have done the same thing," Theo said. Alex felt her eyes begin to water. She had always wondered if the people around her thought she was insane to pursue photography the way she had, but Theo got it. He got her.

"First I took as many pictures as I thought was humanly possible, and then I began to study technique. I took a few online courses, and not long after entering the photography world, I found and fell in love with everything Jacques and his team does. It called to me. Ridiculous, right?"

Theo shook his head. "We all have our talents and callings in life. You should feel blessed that you found yours."

He couldn't have answered any better. As she melted into his arms, she realized she needed to do something to keep her head, which she was in grave danger of losing.

"Anyway, so that's why Jacques," Alex said with a laugh to try to lighten the mood. "I bet that was more than what you bargained for when you asked the question."

"Thank you," Theo said with a straight face and a true sincerity.

Alex's breath caught when she looked up at him and realized how closes their faces were. If she just leaned a little....

"We're back," Theo said as they got to one of the backdoors of the castle. She assumed it was the same one they'd come out of.

"Right," Alex said while she half climbed out of Theo's arms and finished getting down as he let her go. She looked down at the shoes and mask she managed to hang onto all night and realized Theo was missing his mask.

"I should have offered to carry your mask. We must have left it back at the wall," Alex said as she bit her lip.

"I left it on purpose. I think this is the last foray I'll be taking in this world."

"Time to grow up?" Alex asked as she took off his suit jacket and handed it back to him. She wouldn't admit, not even to herself, that her arms were like lead as she maneuvered out of the jacket she never wanted to stop wearing. Taking it off signified the night was really over, and just like all fairy tales, the end came too soon.

"Something like that," Theo said. He took a step back as he scanned the castle wall behind her. His eyes were alert and she knew his mind was going at a million miles a minute. What she wouldn't give to hear what he was thinking.

"Good night, Alex," he said, before opening the door and letting her in. The lights turned on as the door closed, and she realized he was still on the other side. It was probably for the best.

It wasn't until the next morning when her Theo-induced fog had dissipated that Alex realized Jane had disappeared some time during the night before. She'd need to ask her about it. But not before she got some food in her system. Alex was pretty sure her growling stomach was what had awakened her.

With her breakfast cart was a note from Daniel saying that Theo had a breakfast meeting with his mother that they preferred to be private. She wouldn't need to photograph him until the afternoon.

The meeting sounded grim. She stuffed a croissant into her mouth before her worry could eat its way to her stomach and prevent her from enjoying the fare in front of her. If she had to guess, she would say the meeting had to do with the events that transpired the night before, and if Theo were in trouble, she was guessing everyone else involved would be too. How long would it be until her presence the night before was found out, and what would it mean for her future?

"Stupid, stupid Alex," she muttered as she set down the rest of the croissant. She should have never put a party and making friends so high on her list. Granted, she would have never guessed the party would turn out the way it had and be a threat to her future, but still.

"Normally I would agree with that sentiment and not ask any questions, but this morning I'm feeling a bit curious," Jane said as she came into Alex's room without knocking. Again.

Alex groaned. "I think I blew it."

"Blew what?" Jane asked.

"Everything," Alex said as she flopped back onto her bed. "Might as well just stay here until they come to kick me out."

"What are you talking about?" Jane asked.

Alex suddenly remembered Jane had disappeared and might not know what had happened the night before.

"Where did you go?" Alex asked. "One minute we were drinking specials and the next minute I was alone." Not exactly alone, she was with Theo, but Jane didn't have to know that. "Weren't you worried about my safety?"

"For your physical well-being, not at all. But I was a bit concerned about your reputation in the program. I thought things might go south, so I decided it was best for me to establish our alibi. I knew you would have thrown a fit if I'd made you leave."

Alex narrowed her eyes at the implication that she'd have behaved like a two-year-old, but Jane narrowed her eyes right back.

"And don't even try to pull the alone card on me. I saw who you left the roof with. I knew you were in good hands as long as you stayed on castle grounds, and you'd promised me you would."

Alex fought to keep her blush at bay but lost badly.

"What do you mean establish an alibi?" Alex asked, hoping

to draw attention away from her red cheeks. Plus, she really wanted to know the answer to her question.

"I made sure that Emmalee and Taylor saw both of us in your room at about the time everyone from the roof rushed out to the wall. I'm just glad I made the right call staying here since you very well could have been the one to fall from that wall."

"Give me a little credit. I didn't even climb the wall. It was an idiotic move. And what do you mean they saw *both* of us?"

"I've always been good with shadow puppets and impressions. I drew them out, they saw us, we have an alibi," Jane said.

"Seriously?" Alex asked. Her shot at the job was safe?

"Seriously."

Alex thought about throwing her arms around Jane, but after her last hug's reception, she opted for a grin of gratitude instead. "And here I thought you were secretly rooting against me."

Jane's eyebrows knit together. "What would make you think that?"

"I guess I thought you thought my dreams were stupid."

Jane shook her head. "I'm always on your side."

Alex rolled her eyes because it was either that or deal with the one moment Jane was showing emotion, and that was weird.

The door to Alex's room slammed open again, and this time Jewel walked through the doorway. Jane had pushed Alex behind her and taken a defensive stance. "This is why people should knock," Alex said with her voice muffled against the bed.

"I'm going to chalk that move up to your princess status and carry on because I'm too tired to deal with anything until...caffeine!" She ran to Alex's breakfast cart and drank straight from the pot of hot chocolate Alex ordered every morning.

"That's not...." Alex started.

"I know," Jewel said as she took a break from chugging. "I'm open to caffeine in any form."

She went back to drinking and Jane closed the door that Jewel had left open.

"When did you get back from the hospital?" Alex asked.

Jewel set down the pot and wiped her mouth with a napkin before answering, "About three hours ago. Charlie wouldn't leave, but the rest of us had to be here for work this morning."

"Did you get any news about Reggie?" Alex asked.

Jewel nodded. "The doctors said it was a miracle he wasn't worse off considering the type of fall he endured. He broke his right leg in three places, two ribs, and both of his arms. But he's alive and not paralyzed which, in this case, is best case scenario."

"How's Charlie doing?" Alex asked.

"She's a mess. She blames herself."

Alex agreed with where Charlie placed the blame but kept quiet since Charlie was Jewel's friend.

"I don't know what I was thinking. I should have nixed the idea long before last night. But she was so intent on it, and I honestly thought when Reggie got there he'd be able to talk her out of it. Him or Tristan."

"Tristan?" Alex asked.

"Charlie has a Greenland-sized crush on the prince, and everyone except Tristan knows it," Jewel said.

Oh yeah, Alex had forgotten about that bit of information she'd learned last night.

"She would do anything for the guy. Except for not jump apparently. When she went against his advice I really started to freak, but then Reggie followed her and I thought she'd be safe." Jewel shook her head. "I can't believe I let this happen."

"You didn't do this. Everyone made their own decisions," Alex said, moving closer to Jewel and hoping to give some sort of comfort. "And if even Tristan, whom you yourself said Charlie always tries to please, couldn't talk her out of it, how could you have done it?"

"I had more time," Jewel said. "But I honestly thought this

was one of her typical schemes that would be gone as soon as it came."

"Listen to what you're saying. You couldn't have known."

Jewel blew a breath out of her nose. "I know you're right, but it still sucks."

"Why was she so intent on everyone jumping together?" Jane asked.

"I can tell by your tone you think she's a bit batty, but she's not. I promise. She just has it in her head that us 'lifers' are closer than she can ever get to us. Like because we had experiences before she came here she'll never catch up to our relationships. Tristan doesn't help by bringing up stupid games we played as kids, but I told her she's my best friend and Reggie is dating her. How can she be any closer to either of us? But I think it has to do with the princes." Jewel's eyes went wide. "Please don't repeat that. I'm not sure why I said it. She won't care if you guys know about her crush, but what I speculated was a bit too much."

Jane nodded and Alex said, "Of course."

Jewel let out a sigh of relief. "I'm trying to be a good friend while she's going through whatever this is, but she's pushing me away so it's making it hard." She leaned against one of Alex's bed posts.

"Wait, what are you still doing here? I thought I'd run in as you were running out. Aren't you supposed to be shooting breakfast?" Jewel asked Alex.

"Theo got called into a last minute, private meeting with his mother," Alex said.

"Crudtastic," Jewel muttered. "We're all going to be out on the streets. I've lived here my whole life. My parents are going to kill me." The words wouldn't stop spilling out of Jewel. "The queen is going to kill me. She knows these parties are mine and Charlie's babies. What does an unemployed royal tailor do?" She covered her face with her hands.

"Maybe the meeting isn't about last night?" Alex said.

Jewel dropped her hands to raise an incredulous eyebrow at Alex.

"I better get to work early, while I still have a job," Jewel said. "Maybe I'll be able to get a pass for good behavior?"

Jewel started to walk out of the room before groaning. "My life is so over."

Fourteen

"Yes, mother. I know, mother," Theo had said those same words at least a dozen times but that hadn't stopped Queen Marla from repeating her rant yet again. All four brothers had been called into the "breakfast meeting," but the three older sons had assured their mother Elliot hadn't been involved at all.

His mother continued to tell them how irresponsible they all were, but instead of paying attention to the reprimand that made him feel fourteen again, Theo let his mind drift to the memory of Alex in his arms. Even as his mother raved in front of him, he couldn't regret the night before. He knew holding onto the memory wasn't fair to Elise, it wasn't even fair to himself, but he wouldn't let it go. It was one of the best feelings he'd ever experienced.

"Those girls that are in charge of those parties, Jewel and Charlotte, right?" his mother asked, pausing for the first time in at least ten minutes.

Theo watched Tristan stiffen beside him.

"I can't believe we have such irresponsible people on staff," she muttered, her lips drawn tight and her eyebrows knit in consternation. Theo knew that face, and it wasn't good for anyone, especially Jewel and Charlie.

"I have to admit both girls are good at what they do, but how can I trust them in their decision-making skills when they think a night like last night was okay? Imagine if such a lack in judgment went into my bedroom furniture or..." she drew in a quick breath, "my dress for the anniversary party."

Tristan and Seb exchanged a look that the queen didn't notice before Tristan said, "It wasn't the girls."

"What wasn't the girls?" their mother said as she rolled her eyes. She could smell the baloney coming. This wasn't good for his brother nor the girls he was trying to cover for. Which, by the way, Theo had no idea why he was covering for said girls. Tristan was a decent guy, but the girls had made their beds. The princes were getting called out for their irresponsible behavior of attending such a foolish function and Jewel and Charlie had to have known what would happen to them if they were caught putting multiple members of the staff and royal family at risk.

"The jumping. It wasn't Jewel's or Charlie's idea," Tristan said as he sat up straighter and pushed his shoulders back.

"Of course it was. Charlotte came to me and asked for permission to jump. I just had no idea she was dimwitted enough to choose a wall fifty feet tall."

That was an exaggeration, but Theo wasn't about to point it out.

"That's what I'm trying to say. She had another wall picked out, one that was like three feet tall. Hardly a jump. I told her that wouldn't do and showed her the other wall where we'd hung a ladder as kids," Tristan said.

"You boys hung a ladder from a fifty-foot wall?" Queen Marla put a hand to her chest. "If your nannies were still around I'd be firing them, too."

"Mother, you can't blame them. It was me," Tristan said.

"Then why were the boy that fell and Charlotte the ones on the wall. I've heard many eyewitness accounts."

Theo looked to his brother and saw that his fingers had gone white with how hard he was holding the chair he was seated on. Why was Tristan so invested in this? If it were Seb, Theo would have said it was because he had a crush on one of the girls, but Tristan was normally less emotionally driven. Besides, a crush on either girl would spell disaster. Their mother would have a fit if any of them dated the staff. Theo didn't see the problem with it, but the queen had drilled into their heads that there needed to be a line between staff and family. Dating the staff would be crossing that line. But saving the girls obviously meant a lot to Tristan, so Theo had but one option.

"I was there when Tristan told Charlotte to move the jump to the taller wall," Theo said before he could internalize the ramifications of his actions. "Charlotte wasn't sure so she and Reggie went up on the wall first to make sure it was safe for everyone. She was saving Tristan from jumping."

Tristan nodded in gratitude toward Theo since the queen's attention was no longer on Tristan and it was fully engaged on Theo.

"But she was yelling things about unity," she said.

"That was why she wanted the activity in the first place, but the location was all me. I think I must have convinced her too well that it was safe, because she was very invested after my speech. But you can't blame her. She'd fallen for my wit and charm," Tristan said. That last line may have saved Tristan's friends' jobs.

"Like every other girl in the country," Queen Marla muttered. "What kind of fluff do you have in that head to think that any of this was a good idea? You could have gotten that boy killed and Charlotte on top of it. How could you have lived with yourself? And do you know what kind of a raging news storm information like that would unleash on our position, our family?" Her voice had gotten louder with every word.

"I wasn't thinking about any of that," Tristan said. He had lowered his eyes, but Theo could read the relief in his shoulders.

"Of course you weren't. You boys need to grow up." The lecture went on and on, but since the princes were grown men, there was little else their mother could do. This was actually the first time she'd been this upset with them since they were teenagers. But then again, the stunt the night before was akin to the type of scrapes they were involved with as teenagers. His mother was right. They, especially Theo, needed to grow up.

"And you're the crown prince." She turned to Theo. "If anyone knew you were there. I don't know how you escaped notice, but everyone I asked for an account of the night only talked about Seb and Tristan. I'm sure some might have suspected you were the man under the third lion mask, but no one knows for sure."

"It was a mistake. It won't happen again," Theo said.

"Oh. I know it won't," she said before adding, "why did Elise have to leave? She's the kind of influence you need in your life, Theo. I know you all think I meddle too much in your affairs. I know that if we were a normal family you three would have already moved out and not come home as often as you do, especially from your military service." She looked from Tristan to Seb. "But we do all live here and it drives me mad that I haven't taught you better than this. Please be the grown men you look like you are."

She finally grew tired of ranting and stomped out of the room.

"Well, that wasn't what I was expecting," Seb said as he looked from Theo to Tristan. "Imagine a lecture like that and I'm the one receiving the least of it." His eyes zeroed in on Tristan. "Why, brother, did you throw yourself in the line of fire?"

"Jewel and Charlie are good friends."

"We see them at these parties," Seb said. "Hardly bffs."

"Don't say bff," Theo said with a groan.

Seb winked at Theo. "That was purely for your sake, big brother."

Theo shook his head.

"And speaking of unexpected moves, you backed him up," Seb said to Theo.

"He would have done the same for me. And as annoying as you are, I would have done the same for you," Theo said.

The corners of Seb's lips drew up as he appraised Theo. "Good to know."

"Please don't test that anytime soon," Theo said, shaking his head.

Seb shrugged his shoulders. "I can't make any promises. And now on to moves that I approve, who was the pretty little bunny you left the party with last night?" Seb asked.

"What?" Theo should have known Seb would bring that up and should have had a game plan.

"The girl you led off the roof?" Seb said.

"I have no idea what you're talking about," Theo said, deciding denial was the best way to go. Who cared if Seb believed him?

"You can have your secrets, Theo. Just as long as those secrets get rid of Elise," Seb responded before exchanging a fist bump with Tristan.

Theo rolled his eyes at Seb's antics as Seb walked out of the room.

Theo and Tristan went to follow him. "Thank you for the save, Theo," Tristan said as he patted Theo on the shoulder.

"Mother will be on your case for a while. Was it worth it?" Theo asked.

Tristan nodded but didn't say a word. Theo took that to mean he didn't want to talk about it, and Theo wasn't particularly interested in delving into it anyway.

As they walked out the door, Daniel fell in step beside Theo and Tristan walked the other way down the hall. Theo suddenly realized he hadn't ever found Daniel in order to play wingman.

"Where were you last night?" Theo asked Daniel.

"Last night?" Daniel asked.

"The party that blew up in everyone's faces?" Theo said.

"Oh, right. I was there."

"What kind of mask did you wear?"

"A cheetah."

"You knew I was a lion, why didn't you find me to play wingman?"

"At first it took me a while to figure out which lion you were. By that point I was pretty deep in the cups and not with it enough to talk to my dream girl, and you seemed to be involved in a meaningful conversation with a good-looking bunny."

"It wasn't meaningful," Theo retorted, realizing how stupid his response sounded the moment it left his mouth.

"Right. The meaningful part came when you held her hand as you ran down the stairs."

Theo felt that was the appropriate moment to check his emails.

"It was the photographer, right? Alex?" Daniel prodded.

"I think you had me mistaken for one of my brothers," Theo said, barely lifting his eyes. Daniel would be able to read the deceit in them.

"That line might work on anyone else in this castle. Even your brothers. But I know better."

"You said yourself you were pretty deep in the cups." Theo knew he was reaching.

"You aren't falling for her, are you?" Daniel asked.

"What is this? A high school sleepover?" Theo deflected.

"Liking her can be dangerous, Theo. You need to figure out what you want. It's the back and forth that will cause you to stumble. As your employee, I'm telling you to get your head on straight. As your friend, I'm saying the same. If she's who you want, choose her."

Theo nodded. Daniel had figured him out. Denial would be fruitless.

But his mother and Daniel were right. It was time for him to grow up. Stop pining over a girl from his past and man up to his present.

Alex was beautiful, funny, and kind. Plus, she fit in his arms like she was made for him. But how many times had she told him how important her dream job and future on the road was to her? It was everything to her. And he needed a woman by his side, ruling Valdoria. He needed someone grounded and Alex wanted to fly.

Besides, his mother really hated her. Or at least she hated Princess Alexandra Torre. If she found Alex and Alexandra were one in the same, she would make Alex's life a living nightmare.

Elise was grounded. She was the kind of woman born and raised to be a queen. And she wanted his life. All he needed to do was ask, and she would be the woman by his side. But would he ask?

Fifteen

Alex could have taken lunch in her room, but she decided to join Tristan, Seb, and Elliot in the family dining room. They'd extended the invitation to her in the past, and she'd always said no, but it had started to really bug her that she had no idea where Theo was between eleven and one practically every other day. Not that he needed to tell her or owed her an explanation, but that didn't keep her knee from bouncing with every passing minute.

Maybe Seb knew more than he'd let on before, and he and Tristan could help her piece together the mystery. If there was any upside to being the youngest of seven children, it was that she'd honed her spying and snooping skills at a young age. No one could dig for dirt like she could, especially when she was determined. And right then, she was feeling pretty danged determined.

"Are you here because you heard about the ultimate smack down mother rained down on us and you want to offer your condolences?" Seb said as soon as Alex entered the room.

"Ultimate smack down?" Alex asked.

"My brother decided to take one for the team, although I'm

not sure which team he's playing for considering the rant we endured thanks to his choice...."

Tristan slugged Seb in the shoulder.

"He told mother the wall jump was all his idea," Seb finished.

Alex raised her eyebrows, feeling impressed. "Did your mother know who was really responsible?"

"She threw out the names Charlotte and Jewel," Tristan said.

"And you saved them?" Alex asked.

"It wasn't all that heroic," Seb said, and the group laughed.

Alex couldn't wait to tell Jewel the good news, but for now she was on another mission.

"So," Alex said as she took a pretzel bun from the build-your-own-burger spread and placed it on her plate. Since burgers were the king's favorite food, they were served quite often in the castle. Alex had eaten more burgers in her time in Valdoria than she had in all the time she'd spent in the US. "I've got some free time again thanks to your brother's secret appointment."

Tristan had just bitten off about half of his burger, but he nodded as Elliot said, "It's weird, right?"

"It is. I mean he's totally allowed to have his privacy, but what could he be doing three times every week that he wants no one to know about? You guys are his brothers. At least you should know."

Raise some indignation in them. That should help.

But Elliot didn't seem to care and turned his attention back to his burger, so Alex moved on to Seb.

Seb shrugged. "I wasn't lying the other night when I told you I have no idea. It is strange, but honestly, it's probably something boring and noble. It is Theo after all. The only thing I know is that he was talking to some woman named Charla and hung up as soon as I walked into the room. He never does that with phone calls, so I'm assuming the call had something to do with his secret appointments," he said before taking his own huge bite.

Now even Seb seemed over the conversation, but they were finally getting somewhere. Maybe. And she couldn't give up yet. A woman named Charla was involved. That was something. Well, not really. But maybe with other clues it could become a something. She turned to Tristan who had swallowed his bite.

"I'm sure Daniel knows, but the guy would sooner turn in his resignation than give up any of Theo's secrets. It would honestly be easier to get the truth from Theo himself. It's probably future king stuff that he doesn't want to rub in our faces," Tristan said, turning his burger as if contemplating where to take his next bite from. "Our father likes to make a big deal about Theo since he's the crown prince, and in turn, Theo downplays the role. He's always been a brother before anything else."

Alex's heart melted. Valdoria was lucky to have such a man as their next king. But her heart melting didn't stop her from continuing in her quest.

Alex added lettuce and tomato to her burger and bun. "But I feel like I should be there. It's my job to photograph his life. This seems like a big portion of his life."

Tristan paused with his burger halfway to his mouth. "Is that it? Or is there another reason behind your curiosity?" Tristan asked, his head cocked teasingly.

All of a sudden, the mustard she was squeezing onto her burger needed all of her attention. "Of course that's it," she said off-handedly. "And while we're delving into people's intentions, why, again, did you throw yourself in the line of fire to save Jewel and Charlie's jobs?"

"Touché," Tristan said.

Alex loaded a bunch of cheesy chips onto her plate and sat down next to Tristan.

Seb looked from his brother to Alex with a slight frown.

"Wait, that can't be the end of that. I want the answer to both of those questions," Seb said as Elliot nodded in agreement.

Tristan and Alex shared a glance before standing up, grabbing their plates, and walking toward the door.

"Seriously though. There is more of a reason to your curiosity, isn't there," he said to Alex's back before turning to Tristan's. "And Alex brought up a good point."

"Have a nice lunch, boys," Alex said over her shoulder, and Tristan didn't bother saying anything before slamming the door behind him.

ALEX WALKED toward the room where Daniel had told her to meet Theo that afternoon. The quiet hall gave her too much time to reflect on her actions during lunch.

Dang it, she'd probably pushed finding out about Theo's whereabouts a bit too hard. She was sure his brothers thought she had a raging crush on him. And to add insult to injury, her questions hadn't even gotten her anywhere.

Oh well, the other princes would have probably assumed she had a crush either way. Everyone had a crush on Theo Kane.

Daniel had told her to walk down the east wing of the first-floor hallway until she reached the end, and that was where Theo would be. The last door came into view, and as soon as Alex opened it, she was assaulted with the smell of chlorine. Every wall of the room, other than the one attached to the rest of the palace, was glass, and the sunshine beamed in on her. There were a few lounge chairs on the cement, but most of the room was occupied by the most enormous swimming pool Alex had ever seen. There were diving boards of three varying heights on the opposite side of the pool.

No one else was in the room with her, so Alex sat on one of

the lounge chairs right next to the pool's edge and began fiddling with the settings on her camera. All of a sudden, a head popped out of the pool, and Alex let out a scream unlike anything she'd ever screamed before.

"I'm so sorry," Theo said as he yanked off his goggles and hopped out of the pool. Alex knew she should have prepared herself for a half-naked Theo with water droplets glistening all over his body, but she hadn't. Her mouth dropped open in awe, but she quickly regained her bearings and shut it. No human figure should ever be so perfect.

"No. I mean I didn't hear you in the pool and...." Alex had lost the ability to connect her brain to any part of her body as she stared at Theo's chest. She knew it probably felt even better than it looked.

Get a grip, Alex.

"I like to do a few laps underwater before I start to swim so hard that I run out of breath. My brothers and I used to do it all the time as kids, and I can stay there for awhile."

Alex had finally been able to tear her eyes away from Theo's chest and moved to his eyes. Not the smartest move. His bright blue eyes were nearly as hypnotic as his water dripping chest. His nose. Concentrate on his nose.

"I have to admit, I didn't look in the pool. I was mesmerized by the way the light came through the glass walls and reflected off of the water. I hoped to get a few shots before you came in." That was three fully cohesive sentences. Concentrating on his nose was working. *Go Alex!*

"Don't let me stop you," Theo said as he moved from where he was standing between Alex and the pool.

"It's okay. I can get the same shots while you're swimming."

"Are you sure?" Theo said.

Alex nodded because it was all she could do. She'd let her gaze stray again and had begun to count his abs. Were there ten? She thought a six-pack was as good as it got.

Theo dove into the water and Alex let out a sigh of relief, putting her camera up to her eye. She was back in her element. She spent nearly an hour shooting as Theo swam freestyle, the breaststroke, and even the backstroke. Theo was like, for lack of a better word, art, as he glided through the water. He became one with the environment surrounding him. It was a sight to behold.

She knew she should capture a few photos without Theo in them, but she couldn't bring herself to do it. Whenever Theo was out of frame, the picture seemed empty.

Theo drew himself out of the water, waiting a moment as he lifted himself in the air. The water fell from his dark hair and over his golden skin. His arm muscles rippled better than the water ever had. He finally jumped out, and Alex realized she hadn't gotten a picture of the moment. That was too bad for the rest of the world, because that memory would be forever engraved in Alex's mind as if she had shot it.

"Do you know you're the reason I started swimming again?" Theo said. His water-logged shorts hung low on his hips and Alex turned her attention to his nose. Again.

"Really?" Alex asked. She was quite proud that she'd formulated a response.

"I've seen the way your face gets when you are behind a camera. You're in your element, aren't you?"

Alex nodded.

"It's easy to see your passion for what you do. Each time you're behind your camera, I can't wait to see what you've shot. With fire like that, the photographs must be incredible."

"I wouldn't say incredible. But I do love what I do. It's a part of me. I think I might need it in order to breathe," Alex said. Alex again revealed more about herself than she'd meant to, but something about Theo did that to her.

"I get it. That's how I feel every time I get in the water. Each part of me is more alive. I'd forgotten how much an hour at the pool could do for my soul," Theo said before taking a step away from Alex as if he, too, hadn't meant to say as much as he had. "Anyway, thanks for helping me to remember."

Theo grabbed a towel from the rack next to Alex's chair and began to dry himself.

"When did you start swimming?" Alex asked. She realized so many of their conversations had centered around her, and she, foolishly, really wanted to know more about him.

"I must have been like two? We had a nanny who had been in the Olympics, and she was adamant that my brothers and I know our way around the water. Mother wasn't a big swimmer, but she was a little starstruck by this nanny, at least in the beginning. That nanny was also the one who taught us how to hold our breath underwater for so long. She left when Elliot was like three or four, so he never got into swimming the way the rest of us did."

"Wow. I started swimming when I was four and I thought I started young."

"That is young."

"Well, when you've got big brothers who thought it was a great idea to throw their baby sister into a pool before she got her floaties on, you have to learn quick or die," Alex said in a light voice.

Theo laughed. "Your family sounds as sensible as mine."

The door to the pool room opened and Alex and Theo both looked up at the interruption.

"You aren't showered yet?" Daniel asked as he came into the room.

"Sorry. I must have lost track of time. What time is it, anyway?" Theo asked.

"Two-thirty," Daniel said. "And your meeting is at three."

"This is an important one, right?" Theo said.

Daniel tried not to smile at Theo's impertinence. "They are all important."

Theo left the room and Alex repressed the twinge of sadness that hit her chest just because she was going to be out of Theo's presence for a few moments.

"These are really quite stellar," Jacques said as Alex met with him in front of his computer later that night. The queen had asked for a progress report, so Jacques had asked to go over all of Alex's photos in order to pick a few to show the queen.

"Thank you," Alex said, trying not to yell out with joy. This was the highest praise she'd ever received from Jacques.

"Really. Your camera has come alive here. These photos," he pointed to the ones of Theo swimming, "were all taken today?"

Alex nodded.

"The way the light fills the photo here," he pointed, "and then the void of light here. Incredible."

"Thank you," Alex said again because she had nothing else to say.

"Whatever has awakened this skill, don't lose it," Jacques said.

It isn't Theo. It isn't Theo.

Jacques began to copy a few of the photos and place them into a separate file. "The hiring committee is going to love these. Especially the queen."

Alex's heart dropped. She didn't know why the idea of Queen Marla judging her brought dread. If the queen knew Alex's true identity it would be an issue, but at this point, the queen had no beef with Alex Turner. Then again, hearing about the queen's participation did the opposite of making her happy. "The queen is part of the hiring committee?"

Jacques nodded. "It seemed logical that she would be the third with myself and Tony, my senior photographer." Alex was surprised Patsy was no longer a part of the selection committee but kept the thought to herself.

"That's quite the group," Alex said. What she wanted to say was noooooo! Drop the queen and bring Patsy back.

Jacques nodded absentmindedly as he kept his eyes on Alex's work. "This is completely off the record, but if you continue like this, the job would have to be yours. I haven't seen photographs of everyday life that capture this kind of warmth and emotion in a long time. And the portraits you took during our classes were some of the best work of anyone in the course, past and present. You are on your way to going places, girlie."

Alex bit her lip in an attempt to keep the bubbling excitement in her body. Who cared what the queen said about her work if this was what Jacques thought? His opinion had to count the heaviest, right?

Jacques shut down his computer and dismissed a giddy Alex. She had never felt so close to her goal. She needed to keep her head down, work hard, and at the same time keep her eye on the prize.

In the back of her mind she knew there was one distraction she had to get over if she really wanted to keep a clear head.

Theo.

She'd told herself little lies like what she felt was just a crush or what she was doing was a bit of harmless flirtation, but what she'd felt last night in his arms was real. Too real. Those were the types of feelings between a man and woman that needed to be pursued. But if she pursued what she felt, the rest of her life would have to fall to the wayside.

Theo was the crown prince, and no one knew better than Alex what that meant. His life was decided for him. He wasn't free to travel the world on a whim or support Alex in her dreams. His role was his destiny, and there was no room for anything else in his life unless they could stand by his side.

And Alex couldn't do that. She hadn't worked for years to

get to where she was today only to give it up because of a man, it didn't matter how...she couldn't think about the details that made Theo the man he was. The job with Jacques, going to see places only her eyes and her lens would ever get to witness, it was all she'd wanted and it was within her grasp. She owed it to Lizzie's memory, to the heartbreak Alex had caused her mother when she'd left home to pursue this dream, and to herself, to continue on the path she started.

Theo had to be a beautiful person for her lens to focus on, nothing more.

Sixteen

Theo felt like he'd done a decent job of straddling the line between friend and photo subject with Alex for the past few weeks. Even though he wasn't quite sure how exactly a month-long photo subject was supposed to behave, whatever he was doing was working.

He'd also felt Alex working to put distance between them, or maybe he was reflecting his actions on her. Either way, they'd worked away from the closeness that he'd felt with her on the night of the now infamous wall situation.

The queen was still annoyed with Tristan, although that was a better place than they'd been, which was anger and frustration. Tristan wasn't too put out by his mother's annoyance because it meant she pretty much ignored him.

His mother had called Theo into her office, and his chest constricted at what might lay in wait for him. He knew that was an awful way to approach his mother, but things had been strained around the castle for a while, Queen Marla being at the middle of it.

Since the princes were often traveling or living in some of the other family estates, they were rarely all under one roof together for such a long period of time, and the tension of this living situation was beginning to wear on all of them. But it was the queen's wish for the family to be together in the month leading up to her thirtieth anniversary, and what Queen Marla wanted, she got. At least when her sons were involved.

"Good morning, Mom," Theo said as he entered her office without knocking. His father had always been formal with the boys, telling them privacy was imperative. His mother, however, had relented sometime around his twentieth birthday, and she allowed her sons to invade, even uninvited.

"Theo." The queen was seated at her desk, leaning forward toward her laptop. "Can you tell me why Elise's mother declined on her RSVP for the anniversary party?"

Judging by his mother's face and tone, he was right in feeling dread before this meeting. Avoiding the question seemed like a good tactic. "I thought those were due back ages ago?" Theo said.

"They were. And she and Nelson were coming. But I've gotten an email this morning that says, and I quote (Queen Marla leaned even closer to her computer as she read), 'Since the children are going through a rough patch, we thought it best if we didn't come'."

Theo rocked back on his heels. That didn't sound good. Looked like avoiding wasn't going to work.

"Are you and Elise going through a rough patch? I thought you both decided it was best not to go public with your relationship yet. Did she agree to that?"

Theo thought she had; she usually agreed to Theo's plans. Actually, wasn't it her idea?

"Did you uninvite her to my party?" the queen said with a gasp.

"No, no. I didn't." Theo was trying to retrace his words and his mother's endless questions weren't helping his thinking.

"Well, what did you say?" she accused.

"When?" Theo asked.

"The last time you spoke to her."

Theo thought back to when Elise left the castle. Had he said anything?

"When was the last time you spoke to her?"

Theo rubbed the back of his neck. His answer would not be well received.

But if Elise wasn't calling or texting him, why should he feel the need to do it? Besides, she was the one who decided against taking the limelight from his parents. Didn't laying low mean little, or in their case no, communication? Theo dropped his hand and stood a little taller. He hadn't done anything wrong.

"The day she went back to Litiana," Theo said.

Queen Marla narrowed her eyes, and Theo could almost see the lasers she was shooting out of them at him.

"You haven't spoken to your girlfriend for weeks? I'm lucky her mother was so kind in the email. I would want to flay you, and maybe your mother, had you treated my child in that way."

"Mother," Theo began.

"Don't mother me. I can hear the charm beginning to ooze out of you, and I don't want it to effect what I am going to say. Theodore, I am ashamed by your actions. How could you treat another human being like that, much less one that you've chosen to put above the others?"

"We aren't exactly together," Theo began.

"And that is part of the problem. Why aren't you together? She's a lovely girl. She'll make a good queen."

"But I'm not sure how I feel about her," Theo said, voicing the doubt he'd been feeling for a while. Elise was perfect...on paper. But something was holding him back.

"You can work that out later," Queen Marla said.

"Are you really suggesting I date and possibly marry someone that I don't love or think I could ever love?" Theo asked. He knew royals had marriages like that in days gone by. But not in his kingdom, at least not for the last hundred years. The suggestion was rich, especially coming from his mother.

She and his father were so ridiculously enamored with one another, their love was still featured on news stories from time to time.

"Love is overrated," his mother said, pushing away from her desk, standing, and then walking toward her wall of books.

Theo took a step back. "What? How can you say that? You, the woman who was so in love with her husband, the pictures on your wedding day practically glow?"

"Love doesn't always last. Compatibility is much more important."

Who was this woman and what had she done with his mother? Theo decided to try to reason with her. "Can't I have both?"

Queen Marla shook her head. " Love muddies the waters and then leaves you drowning in a pit of despair when you least expect it."

Okay, this was getting weird. "Mom, what's going on?" Theo said as he took a few steps closer to his mother.

"Nothing you need to concern yourself with," she said as she took a step back from her son.

Theo shook his head. His mother hadn't been around all that much as they were growing up, nannies had done most of their raising, but whenever she was, she was full of fairytales to tell and happily ever afters. His parents had been one of those couples that embarrassed their children with the amount of PDA they showed.

"Love is important. It's everything in marriage," Theo said, adamant he was right. His parents were proof of this on the eve of their thirtieth anniversary.

"And how would you know? When was the last time you had a serious relationship, much less one that looked like it would lead to the altar?" She turned her body to confront him.

His mother had always been a bit up and down with her emotions, and tilted toward the dramatic, but this was verging on too much, even for her. But Theo answered her question anyway. They would get to the heart of the matter at some point. "Never, but...."

"So you have no idea. Love in a marriage can make you blind to the other's faults for so long that you miss them, until they are so blatantly thrown in front of your face that you can't deny them. And even then, there's this pesky hope." Tears began to trail down the queen's cheeks and Theo had no idea what to do. He never knew what to do when a woman cried. "The late nights. Why would a state of affairs meeting go until one in the morning? Why would your husband decide to go to the gym more often? Why would he miss more dinners in one year than in the entire rest of your marriage? Why?"

A knot welled up in Theo's throat. It couldn't be. What his mother was implying was impossible. Sure, his father hadn't been around much recently, but the king loved his mother. He always had.

"Mom, are you sure?"

"Of course, I'm sure. Do you think I'd be so worked up if I weren't sure?"

"But, mom...wait, if you think this is true, why are you still going through with the anniversary party?"

Queen Marla threw her hands to her sides and blew out a puff of air. "Because the kingdom needs to see a stable king and queen. The party gives them that."

"It's all a show?" His mother had always said putting on a brave face for their subjects was important, but this was way more than a brave face.

"What isn't?"

That thought depressed Theo more than he would ever let on. His mother's revelation had been like a sneaky uppercut to his abdomen and he was still reeling.

"So, listen to what I'm saying, Theo. It is high time you grew up. You need a queen. Elise is a woman who will stand by your side and be the queen the country needs."

Wait, they were back to Elise? He wanted to further investigate his mother's suspicions. He couldn't believe that love wasn't vital to a relationship, no matter what she said. Besides, his mother only had doubts about his father, not a confession. Anything could be happening.

But knowing his mother, she wouldn't be rational in a moment like this one. There would be no point in Theo's trying to help her figure out the truth. It was probably better to turn his attention to his life.

"Why Elise?"

"Do you have anyone better in mind? I'm all ears."

Theo knew there was one person who had made his heart want to run out of his chest and made him forget who he was, but she was out of his reach.

Elise was as good as anyone else. And maybe if he tried harder, he could learn to love Elise. He'd said it over and over, the woman was perfect for his life. That was only a step away from being perfect for him. Even if his mother was wrong about love and his father, she was an expert on what it took to be a queen. And Theo's number one requirement for his future wife had to be that she would make a good queen. His country deserved it. It was his duty.

Theo rubbed a hand over his face, knowing it was time to step up to his responsibilities. "I'll get her to come back. We'll date a respectable amount of time, and if we are as compatible as we seem, we'll get married," he said in a monotone voice. Theo always worked better with a plan, and this seemed as good a one as any.

Not as good as Alex, a tiny part of him whispered. But he shushed that voice. Alex was an impossibility. Even if she wanted him, he would never ask her to give up her dream for him, and he couldn't see any other way to make it work.

So, Elise wasn't the best choice, she was the only choice. He'd always been able to accomplish anything he put his mind to, and right now he was deciding he was choosing Elise. He would work until he fell in love with her. He could do this.

His mother nodded as she wiped away her tears. "You can announce your relationship at our anniversary party. No one will see the farce that my relationship is if they're busy looking at the beautiful new future of Valdoria."

Theo couldn't even respond. He was frustrated that his mother could be so matter of fact about something that was tearing him up inside. But then again, she was dealing with her own mess.

He walked out of his mother's office without saying another word, deciding that was the safer bet over staying and maybe showing his mother that he was more upset than he let on. She had enough on her plate.

The last five minutes had become like an out of body experience and he still wasn't sure what had hit him, but he did believe he'd come to the right conclusion.

He looked at the time and knew he had to leave for his secret appointment. But instead of going to the front of the castle, his feet took him to the fifth floor and, before he knew it, he was knocking on Alex's door. He was maybe making the biggest mistake of his life, but if he was going to jump into his relationship with Elise with everything in him, he had to have no regrets about what he left behind. And he knew he'd regret not sharing this part of himself with Alex.

His brothers had told him she was curious about where he went and he knew she would come with him if he asked. If he was going to be shackled to a woman he didn't yet love, he wanted to spend the last moments of being free with the woman he almost loved. Maybe even *had* loved.

"Theo?" Alex's eyes were wide and her eyebrows raised in surprise.

His heart raced at the sight of her. It really shouldn't do that anymore considering he'd seen her every day for more than three weeks. He didn't want to know what that same heart would do when she left for good.

"Do you still want to know what I do during this time?" he asked.

"Yeah. I mean, yes, I do," Alex said as she took a step toward where she'd set her camera on her desk.

"You can come, but two rules. No photos," Theo said, and Alex stopped her backward movement. "And you don't mention this to anyone."

Alex looked from her camera to Theo, and he knew she was weighing out the pros and cons and whether she had any room to negotiate. She must have decided the answer to her question was a resounding no because she nodded and followed Theo to the car that waited.

Twenty minutes later they were pulling up into a drive that had become almost as familiar as his own.

"The hospital?" Alex asked as she watched out of the tinted windows.

Theo nodded. "Not what you expected?"

Alex shook her head and looked at Theo thoughtfully for a moment before returning her gaze back to the window. Theo watched Alex's face, wondering what she had expected. He knew she probably thought he was some spoiled prince who only genuinely cared about the things around him when his job required him to do so.

And maybe that *was* the only reason Theo cared about his people, especially those less fortunate. His job had been to care for his people since he was born, so it was hard to know where his job ended and the rest of him began. But he'd like to think he cared more than he had to, that he was more than just the crown on his head.

Alex narrowed her eyes as she looked at the large gray

building.

"Is the place named after you? Or after your dad?" she asked.

Theo could tell she was fishing for reasons why they would be at the hospital. A hospital dedicated in his family's name would give him plenty of reason, but she was wrong.

"Nope," Theo said with a grin.

"Hmm," was the response.

"It is named after my grandfather."

Alex whipped her head toward Theo.

"That was a joke," Theo said with a smile.

"Oh."

"Why here?" Alex asked.

"You'll see," Theo said. His heart raced in anticipation at the thought of what awaited them. Would Alex understand?

His driver had pulled around to the back of the building where Theo could walk straight through a back hallway that had been evacuated five minutes before and up an elevator that would take him right to the wing where he needed to be.

Theo held onto Alex's hand as he led her from the car, something he hadn't done since the night of the wall. He was showing her the deepest part of him by taking her here, might as well go all in and allow physical contact.

The smell of antiseptic hit Theo as soon as they entered the hospital, but it was something Theo had begun to associate with his visits, so it was a smell he loved.

"Can I get a bit of a warning if there are going to be exposed wounds or lots of blood? I don't do well with blood," Alex said.

She must be going nuts with questions, but she hadn't demanded a single answer since leaving the castle. He wondered why, until it hit him.

She trusted him.

His chest flooded with warmth. He wasn't sure he deserved it, but she did.

"We're going to be meeting Charla. She's kind of the one

who taught me about this gig," Theo said. "There'll be no wounds or blood. No sickness, in fact."

They had just entered the elevator and Alex cocked her head.

"I think you'll love it as much as I do," Theo said.

"This is what you do for fun?" Alex asked.

Theo thought before he answered. "This is what I do to reconnect."

Alex pursed her lips as she pondered that, and Theo led her out of the elevator and into the room where he always met Charla.

The crying hit his ears as soon as he opened the door, and he saw two bassinets waiting. There was usually only one. The hospital must be busy.

"Babies?" Alex asked.

Theo nodded.

Alex looked from the bassinet to a very frenzied-looking Charla.

"The entire floor is overrun with mothers in labor and babies that need to be checked. I see you brought a friend, but I'll have to say hello when I come back," Charla said as she ran out the door, leaving Theo alone with Alex and two crying babies.

Seventeen

Alex looked at the door where the short and curvy woman wearing scrubs had just run out. Charla was probably about ten years older than Alex and, obviously, a nurse at the hospital. So why had she left the two of them with two of her charges?

She turned her attention to Theo, who had already lifted one of the crying babies into his arms. The wails of the first infant stopped immediately. He quickly tucked him, or maybe her, into the crook of his left elbow and then lifted the second infant with complete ease and none of the trepidation she would assume any non-father would have around a baby.

"You're an expert," Alex said after Theo quieted the second baby. This one still cried a bit even after being held, but Theo began to rock side to side and the infant didn't stand a chance. Alex couldn't tear her eyes away, and she knew she didn't stand one either.

"Well, I've been visiting three times a week, anytime I've been in town, for a couple of years now," Theo said, glancing a moment at Alex before turning his attention back to the babies.

Alex's heart constricted as she watched the man smile down at one bundle and then at the other. She looked around the tiny room and realized this was probably to keep Theo's identity a secret.

But why? Why would he spend his precious time doing something any person could do? And why didn't he want the world to know? His father would love the kind of publicity this would bring to the royal family. It was the exact type of attention he sought out.

Her eyes once again zeroed in on the all too handsome man handling two babies like a champ. She could imagine him doing the same for his own children. Getting up with his wife for late night feedings, tenderly rocking the baby so that his wife could get some much-needed sleep. In her daydream, Alex filled in a woman for his wife and was appalled, but not surprised, when the woman in her mind looked at her, and it was like looking into a mirror.

She knew her vision would never come to pass, but she couldn't forget a single thing about this moment. Her eyes and mind would never do the memory justice; she needed physical remembrance. She knew she promised no pictures, but as she pulled out the phone she'd been assigned, she validated her decision by telling herself that no one else would see the photo.

Theo was so engrossed in his job, he didn't even notice Alex take two rapid snapshots of one of the most beautiful scenes she'd ever encountered. She slipped her phone into her back pocket and couldn't regret a thing. Her time with Theo was coming to an end, and although the two of them together could never work, she knew part of her heart would be left in Valdoria. These photos became more precious with each passing moment.

"Do you want to hold one?" Theo asked, looking up and startling Alex. They'd fallen into a comfortable silence, and the sudden sound of his voice, along with the question he'd asked, surprised Alex. Sure she'd held babies, she was an aunt many times over, but not when they were this small. If she had to guess, she would say the infants couldn't be more than a day or two old.

Alex shook her head. "I'm kind of known as the fun aunt. I play peekaboo like a boss, but I don't really do cuddling. Or crying or diaper changes."

Theo laughed. "You won't be asked to do either of the latter two, but I've gotta say you're missing out by not doing the first."

"What if I drop it?" Alex asked.

"Her," Theo corrected. "They're both girls. They use white blankets for the girls and blue for the boys."

Alex glanced at the white blankets and nodded before amending, "What if I drop her?"

Theo nodded his head toward a rocking chair in the corner. "Have a seat and you'll be safe."

"I think you underestimate my clumsiness." But Alex sat in the chair anyway. She was curious to see if cuddling a newborn really was all Theo cracked it up to be.

"Just pretend she's one of your cameras," Theo said as he bent over and gently placed one of the little girls into Alex's arms.

Alex sat ramrod straight and felt every muscle in her arms tighten as they gripped together to keep the baby nestled within them.

"Relax," Theo said with a smile. "Lean back into the chair and let her find the spot."

"The spot?" Alex asked.

"Lean back and you'll see."

Alex leaned back and tried to relax but still wasn't sure what Theo meant until the baby shifted just a tiny bit and fell right into Alex's chest. She was no longer carrying the baby; the baby was cuddling her.

"Oh," Alex said.

"It's pretty amazing, right?"

Alex nodded as she stared at the little girl in her arms. She had always assumed this was something she never wanted. She was born to take her camera to every nook and cranny in the world. This was the life for her sisters-in-law, not for her. But as she held that baby girl, she could see an alternate future. One she'd never wanted but maybe she needed.

She shook her head. Her path was set. This just told her she needed to spend more newborn time with her future nieces and nephews. With five brothers, she was sure to have at least a few more.

"I get why once you'd done this you would come back. But how did you get started?" Alex asked.

The baby in Theo's arms began to fuss and he began to bounce a bit, calming her right down. "I met Charla at a fundraiser. It was a ridiculously posh event, one that she said she would have never been caught dead at if the director of the hospital hadn't personally invited her. Of course, I didn't get that information until after I'd been volunteering here for about a year." Theo chuckled. "Anyway, I was hiding...." Theo glanced at Alex and then cleared his throat.

"From an overzealous fan or two?" Alex volunteered. She'd played his shadow long enough to see the effect he had on women. Most of them lost any sense of decorum and control when Prince Theo entered the room. Not that she could blame them.

"Something like that," Theo said. "Charla was sitting alone at a table in the least lit portion of the room. I decided it was the safest spot and started a conversation, mostly to keep the other women at bay. We began to talk about her work here, and since medicine is something I've always been interested in, I had a bunch of questions for her. She was excited to share her passion for her profession and also to show her director that she'd done an okay job of speaking for their cause."

"Which was?" Alex asked.

"Which was this. The hospital was relatively well-staffed

when it came to the basics. Doctors, surgeons, nurses, support staff, etc., but they didn't have nearly the number of volunteers they needed. They hoped to talk my father into a program that would work with the local universities in trading volunteer hours for elective university credit."

"Did they get the program started?" Alex asked.

Theo nodded.

"You talked your dad into it, didn't you?" Alex said.

"He didn't need too much convincing," Theo replied, but Alex knew he was downplaying the good he'd done.

It was a skill of his, but it didn't stop anyone from admiring him. Because as appealing as Theo's physical form was, it was something more that had women flocking and throwing themselves at him. He exuded an inner strength, calm, and kindness that couldn't be ignored; Alex wondered how she'd ever overlooked it. It made everyone want to stand close and bask in his glow.

"Your story isn't finished," Alex said, looking from the baby she was holding to Theo.

"I kept in contact with Charla to make sure things were moving along. She's helped to implement the volunteer program at forty different hospitals so far and hopes to extend its reach to one hundred more in the next year."

Alex whistled. "That's impressive."

"Charla is a force. During one of our conversations, she mentioned that the nursery of her hospital could use a few more volunteers. The college students were happy to mop and even clean up bed pans...."

Alex shuddered.

"But they were all scared of *these* babies."

"What do you mean *these* babies?" Alex asked.

"Some of these babies," Theo held the baby girl a little closer, "have already had a tough life."

"But they can't be more than a day or two old."

Theo nodded. "There is always a need for someone to hold a baby that isn't being held for one reason or another. I'm not sure what the story is for these sweet girls," Theo looked down at the baby he held again. "Charla found that with these infants, human touch made a huge difference. They were used to being snuggled in a womb for nine months, and then they enter the world and no one is there for them."

Alex felt a tear roll down her cheek. "Why aren't they being held?"

"The first baby Charla introduced me to was a drug addict. His mother had used her entire pregnancy, and the moment after she'd given birth, she'd pushed the baby away. Didn't even look at it. Charla didn't tell me what became of the mom, but I came in every day to hold Max. Some days he was attached to so many tubes and wires, all I could do was hold his little hand. As you can imagine, my dad was livid that I was nowhere to be found for hours every day, but I became attached. Thankfully, Max was placed into a foster home, and I'm hoping he was adopted."

"You don't know?" Alex asked. The tears were coming more readily.

"Charla wouldn't tell me. After she saw what happened between Max and me, she realized I needed more of a buffer. She told me I could only come in three times a week, and I was only allowed to have any baby for a week at a time."

"I can see why you'd become attached." Alex wondered what the story was with the precious angel in her arms. "What are some of the other reasons?"

"A birth mother wanting to put a baby up for adoption and the adoptive parents being unable either to get here in time for the birth or to not be allowed by law to see the baby for a few days. Lots of birth moms never hold their babies."

"It would be too hard to give them up," Alex said.

"For some," Theo said, and Alex was hit with the hard reality that some people should never be allowed to procreate.

"Women who are alone and need time away from their babies before they face the world together, the list is pretty endless," Theo said.

"I had no idea," Alex said.

"I didn't either, until I talked to Charla. But the good news is that there has since been a viral video of a grandpa who does pretty much this same thing, and so we've had quite a few older men and women coming in to volunteer."

"That's amazing."

Theo nodded.

"Thank you," Alex said, locking eyes with Theo.

"For?" he asked.

"Trusting me with this."

The two fell back into silence, each rocking the child in their arms. Alex realized this wasn't something she wanted to give up. She was going to have to locate hospitals in all the places she traveled to and volunteer her services.

"They're lucky to have you," Alex said, breaking the silence.

"I'm lucky to have them. I always walk out of here realizing no problem is too big, no hole in my life or in my country is too vast to fill. I always come away with hope."

She had no trouble imagining that, she was already feeling more...everything.

"Why did you finally decide to bring me?" Alex asked.

Theo turned his eyes from her to the baby and then brought them back to Alex again. "I wanted to experience this with you."

That was all he said.

Charla came back into the room a minute later, but a minute was a long time. Theo had more than enough time to elaborate on what he'd begun, but he hadn't. And Alex hadn't asked him to.

"Sorry to leave you both alone, especially on your first day,"

Charla said to Alex. "But it looks like you're a natural." She smiled.

"Thank you, but I think it's more of a testament to the skill of my teacher," Alex said.

"He is our best volunteer," Charla said.

"She says that to everyone. I heard you telling Harold's wife the same thing two weeks ago," Theo pointed out.

"I said Harold was our greatest volunteer. You're the best," Charla corrected.

"So, you have a different variation on practically the same word for all of us?" Theo asked with a grin.

"You've caught me," Charla said, matching Theo's smile. "Your time is up."

"Do you need me to stay any longer?" Theo asked.

"And have your father knocking down the door asking where you are?"

"The king knows you're here?" Alex asked.

"The king knows everything," Charla joked.

"But he's agreed to keep my secret," Theo added.

Alex gave the baby back to Charla and got up to stretch her back. How did mothers do this day in and day out? She was filled and depleted all at once and had no idea how the adorable bundle of joy had done it.

"Will we see you next time?" Charla asked Alex as she and Theo headed for the door.

Alex turned around and shook her head. She'd be back, she knew, but never to this hospital with this man. It wasn't in the cards for them.

Eighteen

Elise was back just in time for the picnic lunch that would kick off all the festivities. The picnic, unlike the party, was an annual event, but it was usually attended only by family and close friends. It was what his parents had done on their first date, and Theo thought the tradition was romantic, although a bit over the top.

But how could his mother continue this tradition when she had suspicions about his father's fidelity? It couldn't be true. It had to be his mother's imagination running wild.

Theo had thought about confronting his father at least a dozen times over the past two days but never had. If he was wrong and it was true, he didn't want to think about the hurt that would bring. It would tear each of his family members apart, it would tear the family apart. It was easier and more sensible to think that his mother was probably overreacting, so he decided to shove those thoughts away and focus on the task at hand. Elise. He would woo her and make her his queen. It was time for him to step up to his duties, and if he couldn't have Alex, Elise would do.

A small part of him wondered if he should man up and ask Alex what she wanted, and maybe she would choose him? He'd actually been close to doing so at the hospital, until she told Charla she'd never be back. Theo had opened up a part of him he'd never shown to anyone and, although she'd been respectful, she didn't want it. Like she hadn't wanted him to court her. *She didn't want him.* He needed to get that through his thick skull.

Theo thought about giving Alex the heads up that Elise was coming back but decided against it. He needed to see reality. He needed to go back to the relationship he'd had with her the past few weeks. He would tell Alex where he'd be, knowing she'd show up to do her job but never giving her an invitation or a demand. The happy middle ground and the distance it gave the two of them had been a good place to be. Granted, he never felt as complete as those few moments he really let Alex in, but it was better to feel less than to hurt. When had he become such a loser?

"The wife of the ambassador from Belgium just had a new baby boy." Daniel informed Theo of all of the changes he'd need to acknowledge as he addressed the guests.

"Was there anyone my mother didn't invite?" Theo asked.

"Not if they reside in the northern or southern hemisphere," Daniel said with a straight face, but the upturn of Alex's lips showed that she caught the joke.

He needed to stop noticing those things. But it was so hard when Alex was always around. Sometimes she walked in front of them in order to catch the shot, sometimes she was off to the side, sometimes she lingered somewhere behind, but she was always there. How could he get her out of his system? She'd only be around for a few more days. He knew he should feel relief, but instead a lump formed in his throat. He was a blooming fool.

The three of them walked out into one of the palace gardens where the picnic was being held and were assaulted with flowers of every kind. Theo swore there were so many that they smacked him wherever he turned. The garden had enough of its own along with ivies, vines, and bushes, but his mother must have brought in even more. Who bought flowers for a picnic being held in a garden? His mother.

"Is there a florist in a hundred-mile radius that hasn't been raided?" Theo muttered quietly, since he saw his mother greeting people a few feet away.

"We better hope so. Can you imagine what kind of event tomorrow's party will be if there aren't enough flowers to cause my allergies to go haywire?" Daniel was on a roll.

Theo was generally a fan of beautiful plants, but this was too much. Flowers were arranged in huge priceless vases and sat on the perfectly manicured grass. Some were strewn about on the ground like a deranged flower girl had thrown them. And some were even added to the bushes. Even the ones that already had flowers growing in them. Theo walked closer to inspect one and tugged on a purple rose. It fell into his hand too easily to have had any natural attachment to the bush it came from.

"Theo," the king greeted his son with an enthusiastic hug. This didn't seem like the actions of a man living a double life. But a tiny bit of doubt niggled at his mind.

He decided to tread carefully but wondered what would happen if he poked at the situation. "We've been missing you at dinners," Theo said.

"Good to know you haven't gotten sick of the old man yet," his father said in his deep, booming voice.

Both father and son were sans crowns, but his mother wore her daytime crown with, of course, a few flowers in her hair. Theo realized his father was also looking at his mother. "I can't believe it's been thirty years," King Theodore continued.

His mother had to be wrong. He swore the look on his father's face held adoration. She was overreacting.

"Dad," Theo started but was cut off when his dad said, "Be sure to try those mini sliders. Delicious." He walked off without acknowledging that Theo had said his name.

His mother was wrong about his father, not that she'd ever believe Theo or the king without proof. But Theo knew it in his gut.

She was right about one thing though. It was time for Theo to grow up and find a woman to have by his side. It was his duty to his family, country and the crown. And he would have chosen the woman he loved in a heartbeat, but she wouldn't choose him. And even if she might have the smallest feelings of anything for Theo, choosing him would mean losing her dream. He couldn't ask that of the woman he loved. So, he had to let her go. That left Elise. She wasn't perfect for him, but she was right for the crown. It was time to man up.

As if it was a sign from above, he noticed Elise's mother break through the crowd and start toward him.

"It's so good to see you, Theo," Elise's mother said, and he turned on his brightest smile. This woman would most likely be his future mother-in-law. He almost closed his eyes at the unwelcome thought, but he hadn't been trained in diplomacy for over twenty years to fall short today. His heart would fight a good fight for Alex, but his mind would win. It always had.

"Wonderful to see you, too. I can assume your lovely daughter is around here somewhere?" he replied.

The woman giggled before looking around. "Yes, she was right behind me. Or so I thought. I knew you two would work it out. You're made for one another."

"Aren't they?" Queen Marla joined the conversation. "Beautiful, smart, and kind. The perfect trinity for any future rulers."

That line sounded heavily influenced by fairy tales. Where had that influence been a few days before?

"Oh, here she is," the queen said as both women stepped aside to let Elise slip in beside Theo.

"It's a lovely afternoon," Elise said to his mother before looking up and smiling at Theo. It was the perfect move on all accounts. No one could question Elise's manners. She thought of his mother, and wasn't too forward with him. He'd seen worse strategy displayed in the best wars.

"It is, isn't it?" Queen Marla said.

"Yes, and the flowers are exquisite," Elise added.

"Oh. I'm so glad you think so. They were a nightmare to get here. I'd ordered quite a few for the party tomorrow and didn't think it would be such an issue to get a few more for today. But apparently, it was." The queen let out a breath. "But they're here and we're here. I'm so glad you are here, Elise," she said before linking arms with Elise's mother and walking away.

Theo glanced between the escaping women and Elise.

"I've missed seeing you," Elise said quietly.

Daniel was deep in conversation with a man Theo didn't recognize, leaving the two of them alone. Except he knew Alex was somewhere and he felt like he was betraying her by standing with Elise. But that was absurd. He would soon be Elise's boyfriend and, if things went according to plan, much more.

"I'm happy you're back," Theo replied. He couldn't bring himself to lie to her and say that he missed her too. No relationship should be built on a foundation that wasn't lined with trust. And in all honesty, he'd hardly noticed she was gone.

Daniel left his conversation and took his position on Theo's other side, leading him into the crowd. "The rumors about you and Elise are already spreading. Initial contact with the idea has been favorable," Daniel whispered as they walked. "Most say she'll make a good future queen."

Theo nodded. Casual dating, at least in his family, only happened when relationships were kept in secret. As soon as things were made public, a ring would be expected next.

"What do you say?" Theo whispered to Daniel, realizing his assistant's opinion hadn't been asked.

"The jury is still out on that one," Daniel answered. Theo

wanted to ask him more on the topic, but they'd just walked up to a woman Theo couldn't remember and duty called.

Theo tapped his thigh, his sign to Daniel that he needed a reminder. Theo's short term memory was fantastic, but his long-term memory could usually use a few nudges. One of the reasons Theo had hired Daniel was the man's near photographic memory.

"Donna Viardi, fashion mogul and designer. Your mother adores her designs, almost as much as she likes what Jewel creates," Daniel said.

"Donna," Theo said as he greeted the woman with a handshake.

"Prince Theo, charmed," she said.

Theo had never understood that expression but heard it more times than he could count. Did anyone really know what that meant? And was it a compliment or an insult?

"And you?" Donna turned to Elise.

"This is Elise," Theo introduced. He, his mother, and their public relations team had agreed to reveal his relationship the next night at the party. People could speculate all they wanted today, but the reveal needed to be precise.

"Elise," Donna said with her thick accent. The woman was so thin Theo wondered how she was able to stand on such waif-like limbs. She put out her hands and clasped Elise's wrists. "You must let me make your wedding dress, no?"

That was why the woman had made a beeline toward them immediately. "I'm sorry, Donna, but the prince is being called to speak to the British Prime Minister," Daniel interjected.

Theo didn't even know if the prime minister was actually there, but Daniel did his job well enough that he knew it would take a big name to get Donna to leave the not-quite couple alone.

They, or mostly Theo since Elise almost always stood silently by his side, continued to talk to what must have been every dignitary on the planet before they were finally able to get a small plate of something to eat. Elise had again done all the right things at the right times. Powerful men and women liked to be heard. Theo was sure they appreciated Elise only responding to what they said, when they wanted it, and always keeping a smile on her face.

After Theo, Elise, and Daniel had gotten some food, Theo glanced around the table where they sat. They were under a white tent in the middle of the open lawn. Elise had turned her attention to her phone the moment they'd taken their seats, but she wasn't the woman he was looking for.

"She said something about experimenting with a long-range lens after she'd witnessed one too many couple-like gestures." Daniel nodded toward Elise as he whispered to Theo the answer to the question he hadn't asked. Theo knew this was Daniel's not-so-timid way of saying Alex was as interested in him as he was in her. Daniel was saying Alex couldn't stand seeing him with Elise, but this was one case where Daniel was wrong. He may have been an expert at reading Theo, but they both knew he wasn't quite as skilled when it came to the fairer sex.

"The girl loves her camera," Theo said before putting an entire mini slider in his mouth. His dad was right. These things were incredible.

"That isn't the only thing she loves. And you aren't the only one in denial," Daniel said.

"So, she's your vote then?" Theo asked as he glanced at a still phone-absorbed Elise.

"My vote isn't the one that counts. What's yours?" Daniel said.

Theo just shook his head and went in for the other slider. It would take ages to explain the whole thing to Daniel, and in the end, telling Daniel everything would help nothing.

"You're back," Seb said as he and Elliot plopped down on the seats next to Elise. "I'm assuming for good, if the rumors are correct."

Elise didn't even look in Seb's direction as she texted on her phone and daintily picked at the food on the plate Theo had served her.

"Let me be the first to offer congratulations and luck, brother," Seb said as he stood and pulled a confused looking Elliot up behind him. "You're going to need it."

Elise looked up at that and said, "Thank you."

Seb rolled his eyes and Elliot looked from both of his brothers to Elise before he and Seb walked away.

Theo didn't think the woman was actually dense enough to think what his brother had said was a compliment, and why had she ignored him in the first place? Maybe she thought it was the best way to deal with the subject matter Seb had brought up since she'd been told by his PR team to neither confirm nor deny any rumors? She wouldn't snub his brother on purpose. Elise was the epitome of propriety.

"You could have told my brother the truth," Theo said to Elise. He wanted to see how she would react.

"The truth about what?" Elise said, finally putting her phone down.

"He asked if the rumors were true," Theo said.

"He said that? I thought he offered his congratulations," Elise said with a pleasant smile.

That made sense. She'd been so involved in her texting that she didn't even notice Seb had arrived. That would hurt his poor little brother's ego, but he could use being knocked down a few notches. Theo couldn't wait to tell Seb the reason Elise had ignored him.

Daniel looked from Theo to Elise and his eyebrows were pinched. Theo wasn't quite as good at reading Daniel as the other way around, but he knew that look meant the guy was concerned. He looked like he was going to say something but instead stood.

"I think we're done with the meet and greet, at least for the day," Daniel said.

Theo nodded, his memory bank and feet grateful for the break.

"I've got some stuff to take care of, but I'll check in with you in a few hours?" he continued.

"Sure," Theo said. It wasn't often that Daniel didn't give him a rundown of everything he'd be doing in the time they were apart. Daniel said it was so Theo would never have to go a moment without his right hand. Theo would never tell him this, but Daniel was actually more essential to him than his right hand ever had been.

Daniel gave Elise one more look before walking away.

Elise had returned to her phone and seemed to have missed Daniel's exit. Theo sensed he'd be having a lot of quiet moments in the future.

Nineteen

Alex immersed herself in a nook between two bushes shaped like the two parts of the Valdorian crest. There was just enough growth around her nook that she was able to go unnoticed but still get her camera out to capture what was going on around her. She'd followed the new happy couple for a few hours before even her professionalism couldn't keep her strong enough to stomach another flirty gesture.

Hadn't it just been a couple of days since Theo took her to a spot that, what were his words, revealed himself? Of course they weren't in a relationship, that would never work, but it would be nice if he would pine for her the same way she pined for him.

She wasn't being fair. He needed to find a wife and she wanted him to be happy, she just wished she didn't have to witness or document it. For posterity. Their posterity. Images of Theo rocking his baby with Elise came to her mind. Her stomach roiled at the thought.

Why did it have to be her? Of all the women in the world, really? And the worst part of it all was that she couldn't tell Theo a thing about Elise's true colors without revealing her own past.

But Alex would tell him. She had to. Even if it made her

seem petty and jealous. She'd tell everyone her real identity as soon as she landed the job, and then she'd tell Theo exactly who Elise really was. She just had to know she was getting the job based on her own merits and not her royal family's influence.

But would he care? Alex shook her head. It wasn't up to her to decide. She wouldn't feel right not warning him, but she could only control what she did and how she did it. Theo was a grown man and could make his own decisions. But she'd make sure he had all the facts.

She felt a bit better and pulled out her camera, to which she'd attached a wide-angle zoom lens for capturing the moments of today without hovering, or puking. It was always easy to find Prince Theo. He was sure to be in the center of the most engaged crowd. She didn't know what it was about the man, well she did, but she was done thinking about his qualities that drew them in, drew her in. Her mind was a messy place. But needless to say, it was easy to find him.

The people around him usually gave him a good amount of space, and it was a simple task for Alex to capture what she needed of the day. She caught moments of him with every foreign dignitary he spoke to and even made sure to get Elise in the shot for some of them. As he spoke to one for a particularly long time, she stepped out of her nook to capture some of the beauty around her.

The flowers in the garden were insane. Alex wondered if Queen Marla had robbed every other garden in a fifty-mile radius of its flowers in order to outfit this garden the way it was. She imagined all the naked gardens in Valdoria and began to chuckle.

Where she stood was her favorite of the Valdorian castle gardens because it was next to the dazzling blue pond. Most ponds Alex had seen were brown with a tinge of green, a few a little better nearing an almost hazel, but this pond was a brilliant blue like the Caribbean ocean or like Theo's eyes. Way to bring her thoughts back to the prince.

She focused again on the scenery. In front of the pond was a pure white gazebo that was maintained as well as the rest of the castle, since it was the place King Theodore proposed to Queen Marla. The three sides of the gardens without the pond were lined with perfectly trimmed hedges and bushes that stood higher than even the tallest man at the picnic. In the center stood a massive white tent under which were enough tables and chairs to seat the enormous guest list, and a buffet with so many choices, the term picnic was a bit too light for the fare that was served. She clicked her camera a few dozen times before scanning the crowd again for Theo.

This time she found Theo at the canapé table. As she drew the camera to her eye, she saw that he was helping Elise to place things on her plate. That was the kind of man he was. He was important, but that didn't mean he left the little things to the "little" people.

Alex let out a sigh. Elise put her hand on Theo's forearm and began to giggle. Alex dropped her camera. She had enough shots for the day. Posterity didn't need to know what kind of food was eaten.

She went back into her nook and leaned against the pokey branches while taking in the sights around her again. Her colleagues were dotted around the party, looking like they fit in except for the monster cameras they all wore around their necks. Jane and Taylor stood unhappily by an arch of flowers set up in front of the pond since they were in charge of the photo booth, a trend the queen couldn't have a party without. She couldn't see him now, but she knew Jacques was also around somewhere.

Everyone looked spectacular, most of the male guests wore light colored button-ups and the women all in white dresses.

Alex looked down at her own and hoped she wasn't getting any stains on it because Jewel would kill her.

She saw Queen Marla talking to a server who seemed to be getting an earful. That was the problem with trying to find perfection in the things that didn't matter. If that became the goal above all, there would never be time to enjoy life. She wondered if the queen had even noticed how beautifully her vision had come to life.

Alex turned away from the queen and caught sight of a button up shirt that looked between yellow and green, a nondescript color that was more like what one would find in a baby's diaper. Her ex, Pedro, had loved that color. As Alex continued to watch the man wearing the shirt, she realized he didn't just have Pedro's taste in colors, his hair curled at the nape of his neck in the same way.

She put her camera up to her eye to get a closer look, just as the man turned around. Alex gasped as she stumbled back into the bushes. It *was* Pedro. What was he doing here? She doubted he was invited, considering he wasn't only her ex, but also Elise's.

Thankfully Pedro hadn't seen her in her hiding spot since he hadn't looked up from his phone. She was about to step forward again when Pedro looked up and then scanned the garden. Alex ducked behind the biggest bunch of branches, hoping he wouldn't notice her. She realized too late what someone might think if they caught her skulking around in the bushes. What had she been thinking in choosing this as her spot to wait out the rest of the party?

Without observing her, Pedro turned in the opposite direction, toward the white tent where Theo and Elise were, so Alex stepped out of the bushes and quickly walked toward a large group of people with whom she could blend in. As soon as she was close enough to the group that no one looking at them would think she stood out, but far enough that no one within the group would wonder why she was there, she tried to find Pedro again.

He wasn't where he'd been standing and he hadn't gone to the tent. That was probably a good thing. She couldn't imagine anyone, especially the queen, would be happy that Elise's ex had crashed the party.

Speaking of the tent, Elise was no longer sitting at the same table with Theo. Theo sat with a man Alex had seen him conversing with earlier in the day. Alex put her camera up to her eye and hoped the scope would help her to see what her naked eye was missing.

She caught a tiny bit of Pedro's ugly shirt going around a corner that took him out of the square garden, where the shrubs now blocked him from view. Without even thinking, Alex walked toward where she'd last seen Pedro as fast as she could manage without attracting any attention. She stopped before turning the last corner she'd seen Pedro take and was grateful she did as she heard whispered voices.

Alex pressed her body against the bushes as nonchalantly as she dared, since the party attendees could still see her, and angled her head as close to the conversation as she could without revealing herself. She couldn't help the smile on her face. This reminded her of the days she'd done the same thing to her big brothers.

"No, but what are you doing here now?" Alex heard Elise's angry whisper.

"The thought of him with you, I couldn't. I had to come," Pedro said, his voice sounding calm and a bit whiny.

"You knew this was the way it was going to work. How am I supposed to explain your presence?" Elise retorted.

"No one knows who I am. I used Martin's invitation. His whole family was going to decline, so they let me come in his place."

"So, Martin and his family know you're here," Elise said.

"Yeah."

"Won't they think you wanting to come to the series of events where your ex is being announced as the girlfriend to the crown prince of Valdoria a little strange?"

Pedro didn't answer.

The guy was still hung up on Elise. Alex didn't see why, but to each their own. It was then that she realized she hadn't felt any hurt, or any other emotion, when she'd seen Pedro. Not even now when it was obvious he wouldn't let Elise go. He would love Elise in a way he never loved her, and Alex no longer cared. She hugged her camera to her. She was free.

"You need to leave," Elise said.

"No."

"Ugh!" Elise's voice came followed by a soft slapping sound, and Alex wondered if Elise or Pedro had covered the loud noise coming from Elise's mouth.

There was a pause for a few moments before Elise spoke again.

"The plan will never work unless people believe we are broken up."

Believe? That seemed like a strange way to say something that was a fact.

"I didn't agree to this," Pedro said.

"Someone had to make the necessary sacrifice when you stupidly invested every cent of your millions in a startup that failed. Who puts all of their literal dollars in one basket?" The disgust in Elise's voice was as thick as the mud Alex was avoiding stepping in.

Pedro didn't respond, but Alex wanted to cut in. Pedro was broke? The guy had a trust fund most of his friends were green with envy about. His parents would kill him if they knew he lost everything. They'd disown him and he'd be penniless and alone.

"It was the best idea I'd ever heard and they needed twenty million in capital. The smartest thing was to front the entire twenty or I would have been sharing equity with multiple investors," Pedro finally said.

"Now you have all the equity in a company that is worth nothing! And this is why you should have gotten a degree in business instead of renaissance art. Useless," Elise muttered before sighing deeply. "Anyway, what you're saying doesn't change the fact that we are poor, and since you are evidently too stupid to recover what you've lost, I have to."

"Why can't you marry some old guy with money," Pedro said. "Did you have to choose someone so good looking?"

The guy was so vain. Of course that would be his major insecurity and hang up in all of this. Alex had never met a man who spent more time or money on his appearance.

"Anyone who's rich will be smart enough to saddle me with an iron clad prenuptial agreement. The only person rich enough to cover what we need, who wouldn't ask for one, is a Valdorian prince. Their family hasn't required one in hundreds of years and no one has gotten divorced. Now it's a tradition that must be kept. Mother has worked her tail off to get the queen on my side, so you better not mess this up."

Wait. Hold up. Alex had gotten caught up in the story and hadn't stopped to realize what this meant. Elise was using Theo? Who was stupid and blind enough to use a man like Theo in order to end up with a man like Pedro? The whole thing was unbelievable. But then again, Alex had wondered why Elise had pursued Theo. Even with her sinister ways, she'd seemed genuinely in love with Pedro.

"What if you decide you want to stay with him?" Pedro had moved from a small whine to that annoying cartoon little boy that didn't stop with the high-pitched voice. What had Alex ever seen in the guy?

"For some unknown reason, I'm madly in love with you," Elise said in a tone that made Alex realize she was probably questioning her choice as well. But there it was. Elise was loyal to someone even if she had been the worst friend of all time. "I need you. And it will only be a year. Long enough that no one will second guess the genuine quality of the marriage. I'll get the cash they'll surely offer me to keep quiet and out of their hair, and I'll be back to you."

They were both quiet and then she heard Elise giggle. Gross.

"Besides, do you think I like being the sweet little maiden at the prince's side? That would be my life if I stayed here. I couldn't stand it."

Alex felt the water she'd chugged down in the heat gurgle in her stomach. Elise and Pedro's twisted love was going to take another person down. It brought Alex back to the moment when Pedro stomped on her heart and dumped her in front of his friends and a smiling Elise. What they had planned for Theo would be an even more public humiliation. Like Elise said, the Valdorian royal family didn't do divorce. This would bring shame to the family and cause people to question whether Theo really was the right choice for the crown.

And he was. If Alex had learned one thing in her time in Valdoria, it was that the people couldn't ask for a better man than Theo as their next king. He was the kind of leader the world needed more of.

She had to tell him. Alex pushed off of the bushes. She could say she was following Elise to try to get a few solo photos when she overheard their conversation.

She was about to take her first step forward when she collided into Pedro who must have just come around the corner. When his eyes met hers, they were wide. Good, let him be afraid.

Elise came around the same corner a moment later, and as soon as she assessed the situation, her eyes were as big as Pedro's. But she schooled her features quickly.

"What are you doing here?" Elise said with a cock of her

head, much more like the woman who'd stolen Alex's boyfriend and nothing like the woman who had simpered at Theo's side. Alex knew she hadn't changed.

"Just catching a few photos and a bit of a very interesting conversation," Alex said.

Pedro balked, but Elise kept her cool and nodded.

"How much will it take for you to stay quiet?" she said.

"According to your conversation, you don't have any money," Alex said. She knew she was enjoying this a bit too much, but she was finally getting vindication.

"I can make sure you get the job with Jacques," Elise changed her tactic.

"I can get the job on my own, thank you," Alex said. She'd played with them long enough. She turned on her heel to walk away.

"Or I can make sure you don't get the job. I hear that three of you interns are pretty neck and neck, and the queen is a third of the committee. If you haven't noticed, I have the ear of the queen."

Alex turned toward a much too assured looking Elise.

"You'll have the ear of no one after I reveal what you and Pedro said here," Alex said.

Finally realizing her defeat, Elise's face fell and her entire body went limp. "Alex, please," Elise pleaded with half-closed eyes. Was this Elise's attempt at humility? Because she had some practicing to do if it were.

"Alex?" Pedro said as he narrowed his eyes toward Alex.

"Her name doesn't matter right now," Elise said through gritted teeth, still trying to look contrite. The woman was a class act. She and Pedro were perfect for one another.

Alex began to walk away when Pedro said, "Alexandra?" She tried not to stutter in her step and was so glad her back was to the couple. She had to continue on. He couldn't have recognized her.

"No, you idiot. She doesn't have the same name as your ex. Although that would have probably been an easier plan if the Litian royal family had the same no prenup rule. Too bad they had that string of divorces."

Hearing Elise act like she could have used Alex just as easily steeled her resolve to tell Theo what he needed to know. Besides, like Alex would have ever taken Pedro back.

"She is Alexandra," Pedro said. "Take away the blond hair and glasses. You know those eyes."

Alex's steps got smaller. Should she turn around?

"Why would Alexandra Torre be here posing as a photographer?" Elise said.

"I don't know. But she's obviously keeping a secret of her own," Pedro responded, and Alex had to turn around.

"I'm not Alexandra Torre. That's ridiculous," Alex said.

Elise walked closer to Alex and her cocked head and smug smile reappeared tenfold. "You always were the worst liar, Alexandra. You probably should have worked on that before you started whatever this is. I think it was the American accent that got me. She's so good at it," Elise said to Pedro as if Alex wasn't there.

Alex felt her breath coming in short bursts and her vision getting hazy. Of all people to find out her secret, it had to be them?

"I'm not Alexandra," Alex said, pushing all of her physical panicking aside and standing up straight.

"Prove it," Elise said.

"I don't have to prove it." Alex turned to walk away again, trying to look a lot more confident than she felt.

"You breathe a word of what you heard and we'll make sure everyone finds out your true identity. It wouldn't be hard. All it would take is one whispered comment. As soon as the thought is planted, you know everyone will figure it out," Elise said, causing Alex to pause and turn toward Elise again. Elise narrowed her eyes and raised an eyebrow. "What are you going to do, Princess?"

Two days. She only had to make it two more days and she would have the job without her real identity getting in the way. But she didn't have two days if Elise and Theo would go public tomorrow. She knew what it meant for a royal to go public with a relationship, it meant it mattered. And if Theo told the world Elise mattered, regardless of how it ended later, the story of what Elise attempted to do to Theo would get out. It was inevitable. And Theo would be shamed in front of the world.

If it had just been a case of telling Theo how Elise had treated Alex in the past, it would have been different. There would be no dark twist to their story and they could have broken up in a widely-broadcasted but normal way. But this scheme Elise and Pedro had cooked up was the sordid type of tale the media loved to sink their teeth into, and Theo would be the one left bare. Why couldn't they hold off going public for a few more days?

But if Alex did tell Theo, she'd never know. She would never know if she possessed enough talent to spend the rest of her life pursuing her dream. She would get the job, she was sure of it, but would the job belong to her or the Torres?

Jacques had told her she'd most likely get it, wasn't that enough? In her heart, Alex knew it wasn't. She would always wonder and her dream would be tainted.

Alex knew she had to decide quickly since she saw Jane closing in out of the corner of her eye.

A smile spread across Elise's face. "That's what I thought," she said as she walked away.

Even after she got to her room that evening, hours later, Elise's expression wouldn't leave Alex's mind. She was so sure of herself and Alex hated that she might be right. How could Alex tell Theo the truth now? Maybe they could call off the relationship in a few days without the truth of Elise's underhandedness coming out and it wouldn't be a big deal? And maybe Alex would be able to find a unicorn horn on her walk the next morning.

Her head fell into her hands. Jane had been full of questions when she saw Elise walk away in one direction and Pedro in the other, but the only one Alex had answered was that Pedro being there didn't mean any harm would befall Alex. Alex couldn't talk about what Elise had said until she figured out what had happened herself.

She was going to be seeing Theo again in a few minutes at a late dinner. Apparently, she'd been the only intern to be asked to photograph this dinner. That meant something huge, right? She was so close she felt like she should be able to reach out and grab the opportunity, but right now all that greeted her was air.

Her heart began to beat stronger as she thought about the repercussions of not coming forward. She couldn't let Theo feel the hurt that she had. Her intense urge to protect him told her everything. She'd fallen in love with the prince. The one man that couldn't be for her, not if she wanted the life she'd dreamed of.

But the fact that she couldn't have him didn't change her heart, and it didn't change her decision. She was going to tell Theo everything, let the chips fall where they may. She'd be outed.

But she could still have her dream job. Just with a bunch of strings attached, the way the rest of her life had been.

She hurried out of her room with her camera equipment before she could change her mind.

Elise still wore the same smug smile when Alex came into the intimate family dining room later that evening. All of the princes sat around the table, along with Elise and the queen.

The king was noticeably absent and the queen was scowling in the direction of his chair.

Alex was about to stand in the area that she normally occupied when she shot the room, but she knew she had to at least try to get Theo's attention before the meal began and she could chicken out.

Alex walked up to the back of Theo's chair and tapped his shoulder.

"Hey," he whispered as he turned to Alex. He took a quick glance at the queen who was still scowling at the chair before turning back to Alex.

"There's something I need to talk to you about," Alex said.

Theo glanced again at the queen, who was now looking at him and Alex. "Could it wait until after dinner?" he asked.

Now that he knew she had something to say, she couldn't weasel out even if she wanted to. After dinner would work just as well as during.

Alex nodded and took a step back. As she did so, she caught Elise's eyes and she still wore the same smile. Didn't she know Alex had changed her mind? That her plan and world were about to fall apart?

The waiters came into the room with the first course when Theo looked down at his pocket. It wouldn't have been a big deal, but it was the third time he'd done it and everyone in the room had begun to notice.

"Is there something that needs your attention, Theo?" Queen Marla asked.

"Actually, yeah," Theo said as he took out his phone. Elise's smile worked its way even higher up her cheeks as Theo scrolled.

"Heaven forbid any of the men in this home put family above the other things in their lives," Queen Marla said.

No one even looked in her direction because at the same

time Theo had let out an expletive that wasn't Theo-like nor dining room appropriate.

"Theo," the queen reprimanded.

He didn't look up from his phone as the sides of his face turned red. He began to furiously type, and once he was done he looked up. But his attention wasn't on his mother. His furious gaze landed directly on Alex.

Twenty

I t was a photo of him carrying one of the baby girls from a few days before. He'd studied the picture long enough that he knew there could be only one explanation, but he didn't want it to be true.

Why would Alex have betrayed him?

But the picture didn't lie even if the news article had. The article praised the heir for his weekly service, the entire thing pitying the poor babies. It made Theo seem superior and sensationalized the lives of the innocents just so they had a good story and the people could have another reason to praise their future king.

He didn't want the babies put on display. He was sure the hospital was being run over by reporters and his overzealous fans.

This was why he had kept it a secret. And in one trip, Alex had ruined it all.

He'd hoped that the picture could have been taken on another day, any other day, but the shirt he wore in the picture was one he'd gotten from Jewel the day before he'd taken Alex to the hospital. There was only one day the picture could have been taken and only one person who was with him on that day.

He shook his head and let out a word he knew his mother wouldn't appreciate, but he didn't care.

He felt anger bubble in his belly and betrayal tear at his chest. How could she? As he looked up at her face, he knew she had no idea she'd been found out.

Theo got out of his chair and waved at Alex to follow him. He didn't trust himself to open his mouth. There was no telling the words that would fall out of it.

As he left the room, he knew she'd follow. He stalked down the hall until he got to his office, waited until Alex came in after him, and then slammed the door as hard as he could. Even hearing the door shake on its hinges did little to calm Theo.

He handed his phone to her and then walked to the other side of his desk. He needed to move. He felt like a caged animal ready to pounce.

Alex looked at his phone and her face went pale. There was his answer. He didn't even need to ask the question.

"Get out," he seethed.

"Let me explain," she said as she patted at her back pocket, apparently looking for something.

"You took the picture when I asked you not to. The one moment I wanted to keep private and you exploited that. There's nothing you can say," he said.

The door to his office slammed open and his mother stood on the other side.

"How could you!?" she yelled at Alex, and Theo fought the urge to place himself between his enraged mother and Alex. "You turn down my son and then come into our home under an alias to what? Why would you want to pry into our most intimate moments? Princess Alexandra!"

Alex's face had now lost all color. But she stood with her back straight, never wavering.

His mother turned suddenly and walked down the hall away from the dining room. Without looking at one another,

Alex and Theo followed. The queen took the stairs up a floor to the guest dining room that Jacques and his interns had taken over for the duration of their stay and threw the door open.

"She's a fraud!" Queen Marla said as she pointed at Alex.

"I was wondering when someone else would notice," Emmalee said, but the queen's glare silenced her.

"I'm afraid I'm not following," Jacques said.

"This girl is Princess Alexandra Torre of Litiana. Did you know that?" the queen asked Jacques.

Jacques's mouth was still pursed in confusion, but he shook his head no.

"Do you allow liars as your interns?" the queen asked.

"Are you the princess?" Jacques asked as he turned to Alex, somehow able to turn his attention away from the irate queen.

Alex nodded once.

"Why would you keep that from us?" Jacques asked.

"Because she's cheating. Her photos must be fakes," Emmalee said, and instead of glaring, the queen nodded in agreement.

"My photos are mine," Alex said, her voice strong.

"Just like your name is Alex Turner?" Emmalee asked.

"Chill out," Jane said to Emmalee, who looked like she wanted to argue until Jane took a step in her direction.

"Litiana. Aren't you from Litiana?" Jacques asked Jane.

Jane nodded.

"The government asked for a special pass for you," Jacques said slowly as if working to piece the truth together in his mind.

"Wait, Jane isn't here based on her own talent?" Cory asked, standing up from his seat. "These two have put the whole program in jeopardy." He pointed to Jane and Alex.

"They're both liars and fakes," Emmalee inserted, and Alex narrowed her eyes in Emmalee's direction as Jane looked like she wanted to rip the girl's head off.

Jacques looked at each person in the room and took a deep

breath, but he didn't get a word out before Alex said, "Nothing is in jeopardy because Jane and I are removing ourselves from the internship and the program. Right now."

Alex shared a look with Jane before both women left the room.

Theo had watched the whole scene like it had been a television drama, his head swiveling back from one character to the other. But when Alex walked out of the room, everything in him knew what was happening was real because his heart, his stomach, even his arms ached as he watched the woman he loved walk out of his life.

Despite her betrayal, he loved Alex. His heart told him to run after her as his mind told him to cool his jets. His emotions, bouncing in every which way, couldn't be trusted. So, Theo went with the side of him that always won, his mind. He needed to take a step or ten back.

His heart wasn't in any better place the next evening and his mind was even worse off. He'd been going back and forth with every decision he had made, and then on top of that, all the decisions he still needed to make. He felt dizzy from all the running around in circles. He was also sleep-deprived, thanks to his brain's inability to turn off.

Somewhere in his head, he knew the lavishly decorated room in which he stood was probably the most beautiful one any of the guests, and even he, had ever stood in, but he was too wound up to even notice. Other than when a statue was perfectly situated for him to hide behind and forget the evening was happening.

Alex was gone. His entire being felt the loss of her, and he knew he wouldn't be the same. He was wrong. His mother was wrong. Everything was wrong. Any woman by his side wouldn't do. Having Alex leave proved that to him. Love had to be a part of it, a part of him, or he'd crumble. The possibility of love maybe coming in the future wasn't enough. Duty was important, but if he didn't take care of himself, no one else would. It wouldn't do for anyone to have a crumbled man as their king.

And one thing he knew for sure, he could never love Elise. Not in the same way he loved Alex. And if that wasn't possible, Elise becoming his queen wouldn't work. It wouldn't be fair or right. Theo just wished he'd figured all of this out long before he strung the poor girl along for so long.

He knew he needed to talk to Elise that night, before an announcement was made. He had to save her from embarrassment and his people from falling in love with her when she wouldn't be their future queen. He'd somehow lost her in the crush earlier, so he left his spot behind the statue to find her.

As his eyes searched, they landed on Queen Marla. His mother had calmed down, now that Alex had left their home, and she was standing, looking majestic in her gown and jewels, next to his father. The distance between them was obvious.

Theo knew his mother would demand the announcement of his relationship with Elise be made soon, in order to take the public attention away from that distance. Dang, she was going to be disappointed in him. But he was a man who had to live his own life.

His father took a step toward his mother and hooked her arm through his. She smiled up at him, a small smile, but a start.

His father's move and his mother's reaction told him he'd been right not to doubt his father. His dramatic mother and her false accusations against his father had made an appearance long enough to thoroughly mess with Theo's head and his life, pushing him toward Elise when his heart knew better all along.

No, that wasn't fair. He'd made his decision. Like he'd said before, he was a grown man. Grown enough to make his decisions and deal with their consequences.

He'd been the one to allow his mother to sway him toward Elise because he'd been blinded by duty, scared of commitment, or any number of excuses.

"You need to read this now." Daniel appeared by his side and thrust the envelope that he'd been trying to give to Theo since early that morning under Theo's nose.

Theo had downright rejected it the first two times as soon as he'd heard Alex had left it. After the next few times he'd told him he'd get to it later. Daniel's relentlessness and Theo's undeniable feelings for Alex wore him down.

Theo took the envelope and crammed it into the inside pocket of his tux jacket. "I'll read it in a minute. I need to break up or something with Elise."

He realized he'd never fully committed to the poor girl. Man, he'd been ridiculous. This back and forth wasn't like him. He'd always known what he wanted and was decisive about it. But he'd been thrown for a loop since, for once, his goal, the person he wanted, wouldn't allow him to achieve what he started.

Should he try to fight for Alex? But she had betrayed him. And he couldn't think about her now. One manning up moment at a time. First came Elise.

Daniel grinned. "That's the only reason I would have let you put off reading the contents of that letter."

"If I can have your attention please?" The king stood in the middle of the dance floor that had taken two weeks to build in a ballroom that already had a dance floor built in.

Theo saw Elise on the other side of the room speaking to a dark-haired man, but he couldn't get to her without drawing attention to himself. He'd have to wait until after his father's announcement.

"I have a gift for my beautiful bride," he continued as a female "aw" took over the room.

The queen's head was tilted to the side as if she wasn't quite sure whether to trust the man, but for the crowd she took a few steps forward to stand next to her husband.

"What do you give the woman who has held your heart for as long as you can remember?" he said. His eyes were focused solely on his wife, and Theo knew his father well enough to know that this wasn't a show for anyone other than his mother.

"Diamonds? That's been done." He pointed to the rocks on her fingers, wrists, and neck.

The crowd laughed.

"Homes, cars, trips, nothing seemed enough. And then I figured it out. What is the one thing you've been asking for our entire married lives?" he said.

The queen's eyebrows were pinched in a mixture of thought and confusion. "A cat?"

"We'll never get a cat," the king said, and again the crowd roared.

"Oh," the queen said almost as a breath into the microphone as her husband put one hand on her waist and the other entwined with hers.

"Evidently I'm an even worse dancer than I'd thought I'd be. I'm sorry for all the missed meals and late nights. But I hope this is worth it," he said as the song that was supposed to be the first dance at their wedding began being played by a group of harpists, violinists, and a pianist that had been brought in during his father's speech. Theo also recognized that the man singing the song was his mother's favorite artist, and he saw her giggle as she noticed.

Theo had heard the story of his parents botched first dance at their wedding at least a dozen times. Before their wedding, his mother had arranged dance lessons that his father had artfully avoided and then, on the day of their wedding, he paid the band double their rate to make sure they never played the song they were supposed to dance to. Thankfully they were newlyweds so the queen forgave the king, but she still never let him live it down.

Late nights and missed meals. His father wasn't having an affair. He was learning to dance. Because he adored his wife the same way the crazy woman adored him. Why wasn't love more rational?

"That was remarkably sweet of your dad," Daniel said. Theo had to agree. The man had hidden his romantic side for a long time. "Now are you going to break up with the witch?"

"She's not that bad," Theo said. "But yes."

"She is that bad. I may have missed it at first, but the more time she's been here? I don't know why you and your mom are blind to it, but everyone else hates her."

"You hate her?"

"Maybe hate is a strong word, but there's something that isn't quite right. She's obsessed with her phone and...."

"You left yesterday because you were trying to dig up some dirt on her, weren't you?" Theo asked as they approached Elise, and Daniel couldn't answer.

"So now that your parents have made their cute announcement, is it time for ours?" Elise asked as she gazed up at Theo.

"About that...."

"Oh no you don't. You already did this to me once. You just have cold feet."

"It's more than that," Theo said, when he noticed some movement to the side of them. The same dark-haired man who'd been speaking to Elise earlier was just a few feet away and his eyes bore into Theo's skull. "Who is that guy?" Theo asked as he nodded his head in the direction the man stood.

"Him?" Elise glanced in the man's direction before leaning toward Theo. "He's not...he isn't...he's not the reason you're doing this, is he?" Elise asked.

The man took a step toward them and something felt very wrong.

"No, he wasn't the reason, but now...." Puzzle pieces from the last month fell into place. The way she was buried in her phone, the fact that she hadn't cared when Theo ignored her, the possessive way the man looked at Elise, and the way Elise looked back at him. His mother wasn't being cheated on, he was. At least he was ninety-five percent certain.

"He's just my ex," Elise said.

"Your ex? Then why is he here?" Theo asked

"He's obsessed with me. He's been stalking me. If you only knew."

The man's mouth puckered and his eyes narrowed in anger.

"Why didn't I know? You should have told me. Why hide it?"

"You aren't going to believe me no matter what I say." Elise hid behind her lashes.

She was right. His gut was screaming at him and he was finally listening. "This doesn't matter anyway. He doesn't matter." Theo waved toward the man staring daggers at him. "We aren't making an announcement."

Elise went from demure to frustrated in point two seconds. Her arms and hands were clenched by her side. "Why won't you commit?" She stopped as her eyes went wide in recognition. "She told you, didn't she? The little conniving...." Elise used a few words that even Theo would have been ashamed to utter. "You don't believe her, do you?"

Her. He could only think of one her, and Theo was sure her letter would explain it all.

"I think I do," Theo said, not even having to read the letter to know that he would believe Alex.

The picture, Elise, the timing of it all. He had a feeling it was connected. He should have let Alex explain yesterday. It was his quick reaction that had him in this mess.

"The guy is my ex from back home who is still obsessed with me. He won't leave me alone. Alex saw us together and knew she could make me look bad by telling you I'm marrying you for your money so that I can leave you and make a life with Pedro."

That was a whole lot of information Theo wasn't expecting. Elise was...cheating was one thing, but planning on leaving him before they were even together, that was cold.

No longer feeling even a bit bad for Elise, Theo took out the letter, not caring if he was making her wait.

He was right. The letter started with a warning, all about Elise's past and what she was planning on doing in the present. He only got halfway through when Elise threw her arms around Theo. "You have to believe me," she said.

There was nothing that had come out of her mouth in the last ten minutes that he had believed, and this move was the last nail in the coffin. She was trying to make sure everyone saw that they were together. If she couldn't con him into being with her, she would shame him. She was desperate, but Theo was even more so...to get away from her.

He pulled away quickly. "Doesn't matter, Elise. I'm done."

"Theo." Elise tried to grab at him, but Daniel stepped in the way. "But the picture. She shared the picture!" The fact that Elise brought the photo up proved to Theo she had something to do with it being plastered all over the internet. He didn't know how she got it, nor did he care. Alex wasn't to blame. Well, she must have taken the photo, but he had a feeling the letter would explain that, too. "Theo!" Elise screamed again as a few of the family's guards intervened.

Every eye in the room was now on them and the one he caught was his mother's. She raised a single eyebrow and Theo knew exactly what it said. Elise is not future queen material. No announcement tonight.

Luckily for her, he agreed with his mom. Because from now on, what she said wouldn't be what he did. He was done with trying to please her and everyone else around him.

First, he needed to finish reading that letter. He had a

feeling there would be more things he'd be kicking himself about and that nothing would be left in the way to keep him from giving his heart completely to Alex.

But how can you make it work? A small voice warned. Her dream, his duty. He had no idea. He wouldn't ask her to give it up and she wouldn't ask it of him. But all of that seemed small when faced with the reality of no longer having her in his life. They needed to be together and then everything would fall into place. It might be naive, but he was finally listening to his heart. And his heart was saying it was time to go after the woman he should never have let go.

Another knock sounded on Alex's bedroom door. It was weird to be back in her family home, but when everything fell to pieces, it was the only place she wanted to be. She should have assumed Elise wouldn't hang her future on the chance that Alex wouldn't tell Theo the truth. It was just like her to do something lowdown like dig around for dirt in Alex's life and leak the photo.

When Theo showed Alex the photo and her phone was nowhere to be found, she knew Elise had to be the one behind it. Alex had stupidly left her phone in her unlocked room many times, and Elise had taken advantage of it. She had no way to prove it, but she didn't have to. Elise had also outed her secret identity, the queen hated her, Jacques distrusted her, and Theo. Who knew what Theo thought?

As soon as she arrived home, her mother had comforted her and her sisters-in-law had told her to fight for Theo. And she had. The letter was all she could do. The ball was now in his court. If he wanted her, it was his turn to fight.

"I'm fine," she said through the closed door.

She wasn't, but she at least appeared so. It had taken two days since coming home, but she was now showered, with hair done and makeup on, and dressed in a princess appropriate outfit.

Another knock sounded. She twirled her hair that she'd already dyed back to her normal brunette with golden highlights. She loved being Alex, but with the dream gone, it didn't seem appropriate. And in all honesty, she also loved being Alexandra. She just wished she could have given Alex a chance to explore the world, camera in hand, for even just a year. Then she could have gone back to being the Princess Alexandra happily.

Alex opened the door and her sister-in-law, Callie, stood on the other side. "I thought you might want to know that someone has sought an audience with your parents."

Alex's heart and stomach leapt into the much too small confines of her throat. She choked on her spit and began to cough. He was here?

"Theo's here?" Alex said around her coughs.

Callie's smile fell off of her face. "Oh, no. Shoot. I didn't even think. I was just so excited. I'm sorry," Callie said.

"Theo's not here?" Alex couldn't hide her disappointment and knew her face must mirror Callie's.

"When we were trying to comfort you, you said it was the job you were sad about losing. I knew you weren't being fully honest, but I didn't expect this. If your first and only thought was Theo...."

She did say that. Stupid, headstrong girl that she was. When her family told her that the letter wasn't enough of an attempt at fighting for Theo, she turned their attention to the job and said that was the main reason for her melancholy.

Her heart felt like it was being smothered, but Alex wouldn't give in to tears now. She'd only allowed herself thirty minutes of silent crying on the plane ride home. And then she was done. She was a princess and a kick butt photographer for goodness' sake. There was no room for tears in either world.

"Jacques is here," Callie explained.

Alex nodded and tried to paste a smile onto her face. She knew it looked as fake as it felt, but that was as good as it was going to get. Jacques was there and Theo wasn't. She needed to accept that and move on.

Her first step, find out why the heck Jacques was there. She began to walk briskly down the hall and the movement felt great. She broke into a full-on run as she made her way down the stairs to her father's office. She knew it was where Jacques would be. It was the place her father always took visitors when they first came to see him.

She saw two men emerging from his office as she slid around the corner and slowed to a demure walk. Callie was a step behind her, which, considering the girl was a trained warrior and Alex only ran when she was being chased by her brothers, was surprising. Callie had to hold on to the corner of the wall to steady herself, suddenly slowing down to follow Alex's lead.

"I wanted to make sure to clear the position with you first," Alex heard Jacques say to her father.

"We're proud of Alexandra and are behind her one hundred percent," her father said as he looked up and saw Alex.

"Alexandra, I think there's something Jacques wanted to discuss with you," he said as he motioned for them to use his office, leaving down the hall with a forlorn looking Callie. Alex knew she wanted to be in the room to hear what Jacques had to say.

"Alex, Alexandra? What do you prefer?" Jacques asked when Alex closed her father's office door behind them.

"Alex is fine," she said.

Jacques nodded.

"I'm here to offer you..."

These were the words Alex had longed to hear for so long. She'd worked for years to hone her craft and she was good at what she did, maybe even one of the greats. But she couldn't take the job with the taint that it now had. She hadn't even done the final test. The portraits. The job was a pity offer or, worse, an offer so that Jacques could further his career by using Alex's connections.

"I can't," Alex said. The words actually hurt as they came out.

"You can't?" Jacques said.

He was going to make her explain.

"I love photography..." she paused. She was going to say more than anything on the planet, but her heart had told her she'd been wrong. There was one man she loved even more than photography. "Almost more than anything else. But I can't take the job now. You won't trust me because of the lies I told and I won't know...." She let her voice trail off.

"Prince Theo explained why you deceived us," Jacques said.

Theo had read the letter! A smile enveloped her face. He'd believed her and had even gone to Jacques.

But he wasn't here. She'd laid her heart on the line and he'd read it. Her heart plummeted.

"I didn't do the portraits," Alex said, forgetting her heart and remembering who she was having a conversation with.

"May I be frank with you?" Jacques said.

Alex nodded.

"It will bring a lot of attention and prestige to my program and company to have someone like you be a part of it."

Alex nodded again. *Being a Torre is a great thing.* But she should have known. Alex didn't matter, Alexandra Torre would always overshadow any perceived accomplishment she had.

"But not for the reasons you are thinking. I have never seen anyone grow the way you did during the program. When we accepted you as an intern, I was already almost sure you'd be the one to get the job. You don't capture photos, you capture moments frozen with the tap of your magical finger. Everything from emotion to vision is caught on one side of your lens and memorialized. What you do is incredible. If you continue to grow the way you have, you'll outgrow me quickly." Jacques chuckled. "If it makes you feel more comfortable, we can keep your photography name as Alex Turner. No one would be the wiser, and your photos would still be acclaimed far and wide."

Alex took a step back. She couldn't believe what she was hearing. He wanted her because of her talent.

"But what about the portraits?"

Jacques laughed.

"We used the ones you took during the course. They were still far better than most of the photos your peers took just yesterday. The committee and I discussed it all night last night and knew you were the only one to whom we could offer the job. It wouldn't be honest to pick anyone but you."

Oh man, Emmalee must be throwing the biggest fit. Strike that, Cory's fit was probably even bigger.

"We want Alex Turner or Alexandra Torre. Whoever you want to be. We don't need the princess, we need the photographer."

"Okay," Alex said, still reeling from the shock.

"Okay," Jacques said as he stuck out his hand and Alex shook it.

THEY EMERGED from her father's office after a bit more discussion and Alex was not surprised to see all four of her sisters-in-law, a few nieces and nephews, her mother, and even her brother, Channing, waiting in the hall.

"So what?" he said when she tilted an eyebrow at him. "Callie would never get all the details straight if I waited for her to tell me."

The group laughed.

"I think I'll see myself out," Jacques said, but a butler appeared out of nowhere and led Jacques down the hall.

It was as her eyes followed Jacques that Alex saw a man standing in the shadows. Between the men in her family and the numerous men that worked in the castle, it could have been anyone. But Alex knew it wasn't any of them from just his silhouette.

She saw the smiles on her family members' faces as she ran past them and slid to a stop in front of Theo. His dark hair was disheveled for once in his life, but he still looked incredible in his button-down shirt and blue jeans. Man, the guy could fill out a shirt nicely.

"What are you doing here?" The tears she'd been holding for two days came to her eyes and spilled over as she stood in front of the one man she would ever love. But she still felt so far away from him.

"You took the job?" Theo asked, looking down the hall Jacques had just left.

Alex nodded.

Theo pulled the letter that she'd written out of his jeans pocket. It looked worn and read, not like it had just been written a few days before.

"Did you mean what you said?" Theo asked, holding up the letter

She didn't have to think. Alex knew she'd meant every word of that letter as she poured her heart into it. She was sorry she'd made so many mistakes, and most of all, she loved him.

She nodded.

Theo pulled Alex into his arms and she'd never felt so at peace. Her tears stopped immediately and her heart swelled.

"Alexandra Torre," Theo said in his beautiful voice, "I've loved you for ten years."

"No, you haven't," Channing muttered.

Alex heard a slap and Callie say, "You better not ruin this moment."

Alex giggled against Theo's chest. Her family was nuts.

"I've made mistakes," he said.

"So have I," Alex inserted.

"But I want to make this work. I know it's going to be hard, but you'll live your dream and get to work with Jacques, I promise. And I'll somehow fulfill my commitments. I am going to make this work, as long as you'll let me?"

To hear the question in the voice of a man so strong nearly did Alex in. Again. What was up with her?

"*We'll* make it work," Alex said, and she barely got the words out before Theo's mouth was on hers. She dropped her arms from his waist and twined them behind his head as she pulled him closer to her, her entire body singing with satisfaction and exhilaration.

"Bro." Theo pulled away from Alex at Channing's reprimand. "That's my little sister."

Alex was ready to fling her shoe, a very un-princess like thing to do, at Channing's head but was saved when she heard four hands hitting different parts of her brother's foolish head.

"I love you." Theo put his lips to hers and whispered the words sending tingles up and down her spine.

"I love you," Alex said, realizing just how wrong she'd been. Her dream was much bigger than a job with Jacques. This was her dream.

Epilogue

Alex stretched as her flight landed in Ontario. It had taken three flights to get there from Tahiti, where she'd been shooting with Jacques, and the last leg had felt longer than all of the rest of the flights Alex had taken in the last year.

She just wanted to be with Theo.

"Tahiti to Canada. Talk about polar opposites," Jane said as she pulled down their bags from the overhead compartment and led the way out of the plane. Jane had stuck by Alex's side through a whole year of traveling the world and Alex was eternally grateful. As tough as Jane seemed, she hated sleeping in tents or with mosquitos biting at her face, but she'd endured it all for Alex.

Theo was in Ontario on some kind of state business, and since it was time for their monthly meet up, Alex had agreed to meet him there instead of in Valdoria. What Theo didn't know was that Alex would be returning home with him.

She couldn't wait to break the news to him. She'd traveled the world with Jacques for a year and pursued her dream. It was spectacular and beautiful and almost everything she thought it would be. She'd shot the sunrise on the Serengeti and the sunset behind the Taj Mahal. She captured the geysers at Yellowstone and children splashing in the waves in Tahiti. But even as she lived what she thought was her dream, a part of her was never fulfilled.

Until she saw Theo again.

When they'd said they were going to make the distance work, they had. They saw each other every month without fail. She'd gone back to Valdoria, he'd met her on location, and they'd even spent Christmas together in Litiana.

But Alex was done with living where her camera took her. At least full time. She made arrangements to meet up with the crew for three weeks out of every year to shoot with the company, and Jacques had been behind her decision one hundred percent.

Her only regret was never getting her arctic picture. Maybe she could still get it someday; she wasn't hanging up her camera for good.

Jane smiled and turned toward her as they neared the end of the jet bridge. Alex looked from Jane to what Jane was looking at.

Alex jumped and took off at a run, leaping into Theo's arms.

"I had no idea you'd be here!" Alex said before kissing Theo and disabling him from responding to her outburst.

She pulled away and said, "I knew you'd be here, like here, but I didn't know..." she interrupted herself with another kiss.

"So, it's a good surprise?" Theo asked.

"The best," Alex said as he lowered her to the ground but kept an arm around her shoulders as they walked out of the gate.

"Good, because I'm hoping my being here will offset the news I have to give you."

"What?" Alex stopped walking.

"I had hoped that we could do some fun sight-seeing here in Ottawa, but I actually have to get on a plane right now. There's a group up north I have to meet with."

"But I just got here." Alex's heart sank. Was Theo not as

excited to see her as she was to see him? Was he getting sick of the distance? Did he want out?

Slow your roll, girl. Alex took a deep breath.

"I was actually thinking you could maybe come with me?"

"I can come?" Alex felt a smile light up her face.

"Of course," Theo responded with a like smile.

He took the bags from Jane and led the women down the terminal and out of the airport, stopping in an airplane hangar where Daniel was waiting.

"Sorry about the change in plans," Daniel said as he handed Alex and Jane a bag each.

"At least it isn't winter yet," Alex said as she sifted through the bag and found clothes fit for the coldest of weather.

"I'm not sure that matters much where we're going," Daniel joked.

The girls left to bundle up and only had minutes to spare before boarding the small, chartered plane they were using since Theo's jet was too big for the small airport they'd be flying into.

"So, my mother says hello," Theo said as they got settled in their seats.

"I'm sure she does," Alex responded.

In the visits she'd made to Valdoria, Alex had worked hard on her relationship with Queen Marla. She was happy to say the woman no longer hated her, but the queen wasn't exactly a fan of hers either.

"She really did," Theo reiterated.

Alex nodded. Maybe their relationship had some hope after all.

Alex had so much she wanted to tell Theo, including her decision to stop working as much with Jacques. But her eyes began to feel heavy as the plane took off, thanks to her almost day and a half of travel. It had been the pure adrenaline of getting to see Theo that had kept her going for the last ten or so hours.

It probably wasn't the best idea to spring her news on him when she was so close to sleep, so she'd allow herself a quick nap and then give him the good tidings.

Her eyes jolted open at the lurch of the plane and she realized they were landing. She looked out her window to see a relatively small building with a snowy white roof. Behind it was a snow-covered hill and even the runway showed patches of snow.

"It's like a winter wonderland," Alex muttered before she was fully awake.

"It is," Theo said with a chuckle.

"I have a meeting right now, but Daniel's arranged for a car to take you to the hotel and I'll see you as soon as I'm finished," Theo said.

Alex nodded but couldn't help feeling bad that this was what their time together had become. Thanks to her pursuit of her dream, their moments together were found between meetings and flights.

Her heart lifted knowing that this would be the last time they had to do this, and she was reassured she was making the right decision. She wasn't giving anything up; she was finding everything she needed and wanted. Theo was it for her.

Theo gave her a quick kiss goodbye before they went to their respective cars, and Alex immediately fell asleep again. The endless days of travel must have finally caught up to her.

Soon Jane was shaking her awake and Alex looked out of the window to see a land covered in white.

"Where are we?" Alex asked as the door opened with Theo waiting outside of the car. Alex shook her head, unable to wrap it around what was happening.

"I thought you had a meeting?" Alex said.

Theo laughed. "Come on out. It's beautiful."

Alex did as directed, and as she looked one way she could see a hotel off in the distance. But the other way was a vast expanse of crystal white brightness, lit up by the sun.

"The light doesn't last long up here," Theo said. "You might want to get your shot before it disappears."

"My shot?"

"This is *the* shot, right?" he asked.

He led her away from the cars and where their drivers, Jane, and Daniel stood.

"Oh, my shot," she said, finally comprehending the conversation.

Theo had brought her to the one place she still dreamed of shooting. He fulfilled her dream.

"Thank you," she said breathlessly as she took the camera Theo handed to her, lifted it to her eye, and immediately began clicking away, all of her tiredness gone.

She kept snapping pictures until the lighting in her shots began to change, and Alex realized it was because the sun was setting. How long had she been out here? The parked cars were much farther away than when she'd begun.

She'd fallen into a photo coma again. At least that was what Jacques called it when all the world faded away and what she was seeing through the lens was the world she lived in.

"Can I see some of them?" Theo asked, moving in beside her. He'd stayed by her side the entire time, probably freezing his booty off since Alex was suddenly feeling the cold.

She handed her camera to Theo and he began to scan through the photos she took.

"You're amazing," he said, looking up from her camera.

She looked over his shoulder, down at the picture on the screen. She'd have to blow it up to be sure, but she'd gotten it. The one of the pure white with just the sun playing on the lines. It was the shot of her career. She knew it in her soul.

"I need to tell you something," Alex said.

Theo nodded and turned to her, returning her camera.

"I'm done. I can't do all of this traveling anymore. I loved it while I did it, but it's time for the next chapter in my life. And I want that next chapter to be with you. And not the way we've been doing it, with stolen moments. I want to be by your side, every day," Alex said.

Theo stared back at her and she couldn't read his face. Why wasn't he smiling?

"Are you sure?" he asked, watching her carefully. "This is your dream."

Alex nodded her head. "I'm sure."

"In that case." Theo walked to a small group of rocks and pulled a dozen white roses out from behind them. He walked back to Alex and dropped to his knee as he laid the roses in front of her.

Oh my gosh! Alex could hear her heart scream in excitement.

Theo pulled a small black box out of his pocket and opened it to reveal the most beautiful round cut diamond ring Alex had ever seen.

Her eyes widened until she worried they might pop out.

"Alex Torre. You did a better job of saying what I felt."

Alex grinned bigger than she ever had.

"But I too want to be by your side. I want you to be the person I turn to in happiness, grief, pain, joy, and love. I want to share every experience with you and I want you to be my queen."

Alex's heart stuttered.

"You make me feel like I'm more. More adventurous, more studious, more open, more understanding. More noble. I can't imagine another day without you. Will you marry me?"

Alex nodded. Softly at first and then more and more vigorously. "Yes!"

Theo jumped up and swung her around in his arms.

"There was no meeting, was there?" Alex asked as she swung through the air.

"Jacques might have given me a heads up about your decision," Theo said, setting her on the ground but keeping her enfolded in his arms as he dropped his head to hers, his kiss suddenly warming all the parts of her body that had felt cold. Who needed a heater when a girl had Prince Theo Kane to kiss?

Alex finally broke the kiss to say, "You little sneaks. I can't believe Jacques didn't give *me* a heads up. I have known him longer."

"But I think he likes me better," Theo said.

Alex pulled back like she was offended, until she realized he was probably right. Everyone loved Theo. They couldn't help it. She knew she couldn't.

Theo pulled her close again and kissed her forehead as he asked, "Are you ready to be a queen?"

Alex nodded her head. "But even more, I'm ready to be your wife." Then she jumped onto her tiptoes to meet her fiancé's warm and all too inviting lips.

"Jewel? Jewel Huber?"

Jewel would have recognized that voice anywhere, but a small part of her hoped she'd become delusional in the last few minutes. Anything would be better than seeing....

"Tristan," Jewel said when the man in question ran up to her side. There was no avoiding him at that point.

Paris was still cold in early March, and Tristan hugged his knee-length jacket around him as he walked beside Jewel. Jewel would never admit it, but Tristan looked good. Really good. His chestnut-brown hair had grown a little longer than usual but was still trimmed and in line with Valdorian military standards. His facial hair was between scruff and a beard, short enough as to hide none of his beautiful features but still long enough for Jewel to want to run her hand across his cheek. His honey brown eyes were fixed on her, and none of this was fair to her willpower.

"What are you doing here?" Tristan asked. He lifted an arm as if he might swing it around Jewel's shoulders, but Jewel stepped away and his arm dropped.

"Paris Fashion Week." Jewel motioned to the building less than a block ahead of them where she'd be watching her next show. Between the weather and her hectic fashion week schedule, Jewel was typically driven far too fast by locals from show to show, but since she'd had an hour break and the next show was just a block away, Jewel had decided to enjoy the fresh air. Huge mistake.

"What are you doing in Paris?" Jewel asked when she realized it would be rude not to. "Aren't you stationed in...?"

"Anduri," Tristan finished for her.

"Right," she said with a nod, hugging her own cloak around her shoulders. Fashionably speaking, a cloak was the definite right choice for her outfit today, but the icy wind was reminding her it hadn't been quite the best selection considering the weather.

But as the royal tailor for the Valdorian royal family, fashion came second to nothing for Jewel and, with her fitted navy blue sweater dress and over-the-knee camel boots, a cream cloak was the only way to go.

"I'm here on state business for Theo. Since he's caught up in wedding planning and all. I guess it's a busy time in a man's life?" Tristan said with his signature grin that made Jewel melt a little every time she saw it.

Of course. State business. Because Theo, Tristan's brother, was the crown prince and one of the heads of state. Meaning Tristan was not just Tristan, he was the Honorable Prince Tristan Edward Kane and way out of Jewel's league. No, not out of her league; they didn't even play the same sport.

"Busy would be an understatement," Jewel said, trying to match Tristan's easy grin with one of her own. Jewel's workload had quadrupled with the announcement of the crown prince's impending marriage to Princess Alexandra Torre. But Jewel didn't mind because she loved her job and she loved Princess Alex.

"But they let you away for a week?" Tristan asked as they stopped in front of the glass building that was usually a greenhouse but had been converted into a runway for the day's events.

"Just for the week. I'm on a flight back as soon as my last show is over tomorrow night."

"So, you'll still be here tonight? Any plans for dinner?"

Jewel swallowed back the lump that had formed in her throat. Tristan asking her to join him for a meal wasn't a new thing. He'd been trying to go on a "date" with her for years. But Jewel had always held strong in her denial of him because she'd witnessed the aftermath of every female heart Tristan had walked away from. "Date" didn't have the same connotation to Tristan as it did to the rest of the world because, for him, it was only and always a one-time thing.

"Sorry, yeah. They've got me booked solid," Jewel said, grateful she didn't have to lie. The designer of her last show that evening had asked to have Jewel join him and his team at a celebratory dinner. No doubt to get his hat in the ring to be able to design the princess's wedding dress, but even if she was being manipulated, she had plans she could use to avoid Tristan and that was all that mattered.

"Even for dinner?" Tristan asked.

Jewel nodded before she looked toward the venue and saw that people were still waiting outside and the doors hadn't opened. She needed an out and she needed one soon. *Open the doors people.*

"Who is your dinner with?" Tristan asked.

"Bagliatelli. You know how these things are. I don't really want to go, but if I don't show up...." Jewel gave her excuse and threw in the designer's last name with a smile. She knew Tristan had been banking on her lying about her plans. He'd known Jewel was avoiding him since her first blundering attempt to say no to going on a date with him.

Because, despite his uncommonly good looks and the fact that he was a prince, as if he hadn't been bestowed with enough,

Tristan was also the smartest man Jewel had ever met. He'd been taking Calculus when the rest of the kids his age were stuck in Algebra, and he'd memorized the periodic table when he was only ten. King Theodore liked to boast that his second son could have had a huge future in any profession, and it was only his loyalty to country and crown that drew him to the military.

Tristan took his phone out of his coat pocket and began typing.

Jewel watched him for a second before turning toward the doors to see that they'd finally opened.

"I guess I should let you go," Jewel said as she motioned to his phone and then to the doors.

Tristan looked from Jewel to the doors of the venue, but his perusal was interrupted by the beeping of an incoming text message on his phone. "Can you hold on for just a second?" he asked, his gaze back on Jewel.

He kept his mesmerizing eyes on her until she nodded in agreement, and then he turned his attention back to his phone.

"We're in luck. Vincenzo," Tristan used Bagliatelli's first name and Jewel knew she was in trouble, "owes me a favor. Actually a few favors, and he said he'd be happy to let you out of your commitment tonight. Since you didn't want to go, right?"

Jewel felt panic clutching at her chest. Why hadn't she built an excuse on a more solid foundation? She hadn't been this close to a date with Tristan since the first time he asked her out. She needed to find a way out. She nodded and displayed what she hoped looked like a perfectly pleasant smile on her face.

Think, Jewel.

"Did you say tonight?" Jewel said as she pulled out her own phone.

"Don't try to say that you had your dinner with Vincenzo mixed up with another engagement because he already told me that your dinner was supposed to be tonight. You've got a hole in your evening, gorgeous, and I'm more than pleased to fill it."

He was right.

"Here's my number, " he said as her phone vibrated with a new text and she looked down to see that indeed it came from a number she didn't know. "Save it now so that you can't say that you don't answer texts or calls from strange numbers."

That was the excuse she'd used the fourth time he asked her out.

"And I'm texting you the name of the restaurant and directions from your hotel."

Excuse number seven was that she'd gotten lost.

"How do you know where I'm staying?" Jewel asked.

"You didn't think this meeting was by chance, did you?" Tristan asked with the sparkle in his eye of a boy who'd finally won a round of the game he'd been playing for years.

"You knew I was here? But I don't usually walk between shows," Jewel said, her mind trying to catch up to Tristan's ploy.

" As soon as I found out you were in Paris, I jumped at the chance to see you. I knew this was the biggest chunk of free time you had and would have 'bumped' into you either way."

Jewel gave a tiny shake of her head. She should have expected a move like this. Tristan wasn't one to lose, and so far, he'd lost every round in win a date with Jewel Huber. Not that she was some great prize, but she was the only prize he had yet to win over.

"And the dinner with Bagliatelli. Did you set that up too?"

"Oh no, that was real. But I would have gotten you out of whatever your plans were some way or another."

He smirked, and Jewel wanted to slap and kiss him all at once. The man was infuriating and adorable. Dang it, she was in so much trouble. *This* was why she'd said no for years.

"I know you aren't here with any friends, and I checked the weather and it'll be cold, but cloudless."

Her friends needing her and the possibility of rain were excuses number two and six.

"If you text me that you're sick, I'll be at your door with room service. And if it's a stomach bug, I'll make sure to skip the food, but I'll be there to hold your hair as you throw up."

Excuses number thirteen, fourteen, and fifteen. Jewel had been in a bit of an excuse rut.

He'd more than covered his bases since Jewel couldn't use any of her other excuses, and in all honesty, she had no new ideas. Tristan had been persistent in his pursuit of her, but she didn't want the game to be done. As soon as the chase was over, he'd be gone and she'd be heartbroken. Because as flippant as she was to his face, she'd fallen for Tristan Kane hook, line, and sinker many years ago. It was the main reason she could never go on a date with him.

"Anything I missed, love?" he asked.

Jewel's mouth went dry and she willed her brain to work. "I'm allergic to shellfish," Jewel said when she recognized the name of the fancy restaurant Tristan had sent her directions to. Not her greatest work, but it bought her some time.

"That text was more just for fun. Had to prove to you I had all of your excuses covered. Do you think I'd let you find your own way in an unfamiliar city? Not with me, gorgeous," he said. "I'll be at your hotel to pick you up at nine. That should give you plenty of time after the show to get ready."

Excuse number seventeen had been that she wasn't ready. She'd yelled at him through her door as he knocked on the other side. The excuse rut had continued and she knew she couldn't use the sick line again, so she was caught without an excuse when he came to her door. Thankfully, as she was yelling that she couldn't go out with him, Pamela, one of Jewel's coworkers, had noticed Tristan. She took him away before he could find a way to deny her or accuse Jewel about the lameness of her excuse.

"But this time, you're coming. Glammed up or not. I actually very much like the natural version of Jewel." Tristan winked and she blushed because she knew he was thinking about the time that he'd seen her getting out of the pool, one of the few times he'd witnessed her sans makeup since they were thirteen.

The last of the line of people waiting to get into the venue was entering the show, and Jewel knew she had to get in before they closed the doors or she'd miss it altogether.

"I'll talk to the place I'm taking you to as soon as I leave and I'll be sure that there will be no shellfish anywhere within the vicinity. Although, I've known you since we were crawling and I know you've eaten a shrimp or five thousand in that time."

Jewel grinned that he'd noticed that about her but then schooled her face. The last thing she needed was to feel any type of sentiment toward Tristan right now. All her guards had to be up.

"And the dress is casual. Or not. Whatever you want to wear will be perfect."

Her first excuse had been that she had nothing in her wardrobe fit to go on a date with a prince. That excuse no longer worked once she became the royal tailor and had access to all the best clothes in the world, including her own designs.

Jewel bit the inside of her lip. This was bad. So, so bad.

"So, what do you say, Jewel? Go out with me?"

He could easily have said; do you admit defeat? Because that was the only reason he'd continued asking her out; he needed to win. And now he had.

Her season of holding Tristan's interest was finished, and Jewel was already beginning to mourn being forgotten by Tristan. But her time was over. She'd slipped out of his grasp on enough occasions and it was time to just get the date over and done with. Besides, Jewel knew when she was out-plotted and out-maneuvered. She almost started to clap at his game well played, but instead she nodded.

"You better get in there. See you at nine, love," he said as he kissed his two fingers and placed them on her bewildered forehead before he turned on his heel.

Jewel turned away and hurried toward the closing doors of the fashion show, slipping through them and into her front row seat just in time. She tried to concentrate on the beautiful gowns being shown in front of her. She would usually be drooling at the cuts, colors, and skill behind each of the designs, but instead she could only think of one thing. She was going on a date with Tristan Kane in the most romantic city in the world.

Want to keep reading? Get Marrying the Prince!

Julia Keanini

Julia Keanini is just a city girl living in a country world (and secretly loving it). She loves the mountains and would adore the beach, if it weren't for all the sand and salt (wait, that is the beach?). A good book, a great song, or a huge piece of chocolate can lift her mood, but her true happiness is found in her little fam. She writes about girls who deal with what life throws at them and always about love, cause she LOVES love.